# WILLY'S SUMMER DREAM

# WILLY'S SUMMER DREAM

## Kay Brown

GULLIVER BOOKS

HARCOURT BRACE JOVANOVICH, PUBLISHERS

San Diego   New York   London

Library of Congress Cataloging-in-Publication Data
Brown, Kay, 1932-
Willy's summer dream/by Kay Brown. — 1st ed.
p.   cm.
"Gulliver books."
Summary: Fourteen-year-old Willy, slow in school and ridiculed by
other boys in his Brooklyn neighborhood, faces another dull summer
with his mother until tutoring from an older girl and other special
experiences help him develop a sense of self-confidence.
ISBN 0-15-200645-1
[1. Self-confidence — Fiction.   2. Brooklyn (New York, N.Y.) —
Fiction.   3. Afro-Americans — Fiction.   4. Single-parent family —
Fiction.]   I. Title.
PZ7.B81559Wi   1989
[Fic] — dc19                                                    88-21876

Designed by Dalia Hartman
Printed in the United States of America
First edition
A B C D E

To my beloved son,
CLAYTON,
and to the memory of
DR. JOHN OLIVER KILLENS and
DR. ELEANOR LEACOCK,
who never stopped believing
in Willy

# WILLY'S SUMMER DREAM

Willy just wanted a chance to shoot the ball, no big deal really, just to see if he could make it drop swoop down into the basket. That's all. It had taken him a long time to muster up nerve to pass the schoolyard each day, make it seem like he was just happening by. He'd worked it all out in his mind, but every time he'd end up rushing past the gate, his eyes locked into the distance. This time was different. He was going to march right in. He tried to ignore the heavy weight in his chest and the growing heat of his body. Then he heard his own voice rasp loudly, "Hey, can I shoot one?"

All four boys stopped, their astonished faces swinging toward him, then away to exchange glances with one another, faces blank, before swinging toward him again. Suddenly the ball was coming straight at him, sailing with graceful speed through the air before Willy missed the ball and watched it bounce a few times, then roll and come to rest a few inches from his feet. Sadly he looked down at the still basketball and listened to the jeer, "Can't even catch. How you gonna play, sucker?"

He squeezed his eyes shut as he felt the burning in his

body, hotter than ever, move slowly up and circle his ear-lobes. The sharp sounds of their laughter echoed in his head. He opened his eyes to see them slap one another's palms, their bodies swinging in hip dancelike motions of ridicule.

The lanky boy with slanty eyes and white-capped pimples grabbed the ball from near Willy's left sneaker, and they went back to shooting as if Willy were no longer standing there. The burn wrapped around his entire body. He turned quickly, hoping he could control his sudden desire to urinate.

Why? Willy asked himself as he pushed blindly through a bunch of people. Why should anything be different, anyway? Still, they could've given him a chance. He stepped over some cement construction at the corner of his block. He could've handled the ball, really. He'd watched all the plays on television, knew the moves by heart. What was so bad about wanting in?

Maybe it's a good thing they didn't let him shoot. Maybe he would've missed. That would've been worse. He felt beat down, aching for his room. He quickened his step as again he felt the urgency of his bladder.

That night sleep came in fits and starts. The four boys did their slow dream dance in a schoolyard, pushing through thick shadows. Willy overslept and arrived at school in the middle of social science.

"Oh, there you are, Willy." His teacher greeted him unexpectedly with a smile. He had to concentrate to get to his seat. He was glad he'd missed math and smiled as he slid behind his desk. He looked at the colored map tacked over the blackboard. Geography, the only subject he really enjoyed. He liked hearing about so many places, pretending he could be transported to anywhere in the world he wanted. But there was Mr. Bates, all of a sudden, with his long hair and all standing in the open doorway, beckoning to his teacher. Miss Willis was nodding her gray head as he whispered to her. She closed the giant book, placing her hand over it like a preacher closing his bible at church.

When she called his name, her voice was a booming echo at the end of a long tunnel. He could have crawled under the desk, but there was no magic, no vanishing acts like on TV. "Come up here, Willy."

He took account as he moved up. No, he hadn't torn out no pictures from library books. And no, he hadn't rolled up his homework assignment into a tight ball and thrown it away. He hadn't even been daydreaming lately. Whatever it was, it had to be bad since he'd been so good.

"You're going with Mr. Bates, Willy," his teacher told him. Her hand lifted from the book to smooth back a few stray wisps from her forehead. "You'd better take your things with you," she added. "Leave your books."

Willy followed the principal down the hallway. He knew if something was up, Mr. Bates was behind it. Supposed to be a good guy, too.

"Don't worry, Willy," he said over his shoulder. "Everything will be all right." Willy knew better; it was never all right. He felt hatred for the phony long hair bouncing up and down against the edge of the principal's striped shirt collar.

Willy suspected that whatever was wrong had something to do with what his mother told him he would eventually grow out of—whatever that was supposed to be. At first he'd thought it was because he couldn't make friends. Sometimes she'd say he should try harder with the kids at school, like he was never trying . . . Or maybe it was that laughing business that snuck up on him all of a sudden when nothing was funny. Or maybe it was him growing so fast this past year that he was taller than most of the kids in his class. It was hard to understand a lot of stuff in school, too. Maybe . . .

It had taken him a long time to figure out that he couldn't keep up with the class. There were those meetings his mother had before he went into junior high. And the other things, like those times he'd be standing on the sidelines and a kid would pick him to join a game, then for some reason change his mind. One time when they needed another player for volleyball, someone said, "Don't bother with him. He's retarded." Retarded. It was a name, just a name that they'd call kids, kids that don't fit, but that didn't make him feel any better, just worse, and he wondered . . .

Of late he began to think something could really be wrong with him. Mr. Bates closed his office door and motioned for Willy to sit down.

Willy peered from behind books piled on the side of

the desk as the principal leaned back comfortably in his chair, a smile widening his tanned face. Mr. Bates was different from most principals, young and the type who played tennis or baked himself on some beach trying to get black like Willy.

"Willy, you'll be going into a special class this week. No big deal, but we think the move will be better for you," he announced cheerfully. Willy could tell right away that Mr. Bates was not going to explain anything. But Willy wanted to know why, anyway. Why right near the end of the term? The principal explained that his parents would be contacted by letter. Stupid. He knew it was just Willy and his mother. Mr. Bates leaned forward fingering the files on top of the desk and glanced at his watch; Willy understood he had been dismissed.

Going home afterward, he wondered how ole Bertha was going to take it this time. There had been other letters, other notes summoning his mother. He was determined to wait it out this time, to say nothing. But by the time his mother arrived home, changed her clothes, and gone into the kitchen to start the meal, he'd blurted out the whole story. And as the onions and green peppers danced sizzlingly in the frying pan, his mother had become dreamy-eyed, quiet, as if he weren't there.

Finally, she looked up from the spaghetti sauce she'd been making, her hand never ceasing to stir the ruby thickness. "Those damn people, always messing with people's children."

Now he felt a little better. That's right, she'll show

them. His mother never took no stuff off nobody—that's for sure.

The next afternoon, his mother arrived home early, just an hour after he'd come from school. She sank wearily into the cushions of the easy chair, hands rubbing her thighs through the thin fabric of her dress.

"What's wrong?" he asked, his face twitching slightly.

"Nothing."

"Well, what happened at school? Can I stay in my class?"

She studied her fingernails resting on the padded arm of the chair. The freshly polished white pearl tips caught the sunlight filtering through the living room window.

"You didn't tell me they made you take a test, Willy." He frowned, reaching back to remember some kind of exam last year. No big deal. There were always tests. He took them, never got the right score, but no big deal.

"Oh, I failed a test?" he asked, with a trace of sarcasm.

"Well, it wasn't that kind of test exactly . . ." she replied softly. "You didn't pass or fail, Willy. You just . . ." As her voice trailed off, he felt creepy, like earlier in Mr. Bates' office.

"They really got some nerve, I tell you!" she suddenly snapped, her mouth twisting. "He should be strumming a guitar someplace in the Village instead of being in charge of a school. And that dumb doctor, talking to me like I didn't have a brain in my head. All they know is what they read in their college textbooks, and that isn't much, I can tell you."

For a moment he heard nothing but the drone of Mr.

6

Bowers's lawn mower next door, coming in through the open window. "Well, we'll just have to get you a transfer again; that's all there is to it," she said emphatically.

It took a few minutes for the words to register. Another transfer? Damn. He was tired of being pushed around all over the place like that. First he's in this school, then that school—why any school? If he was too dumb to learn, then they should forget about the whole damn thing! I don't have to go to no school. He wanted to tell her that, to make her understand that he should just stay *home*, home in his room. The only thing good in school was geography anyway, and even that wasn't worth the trouble. He said nothing.

Three days later a letter came. His mother handed him the card that had been enclosed and told him to go along with the school officials. She would look for another school during the summer.

Try as he would, Willy could not think much about anything that next Monday. His thoughts seemed to fizzle, to shred into meaningless pieces. With a sigh he pulled on his clothes, skipped breakfast, and locked the door carefully behind him before walking the eight blocks to school. He knew he was late again when he didn't see anyone in the schoolyard. He must have forgotten to wind up his Big Ben. Glancing down at the shiny orange card with black letters, he tried to make out his new class number, the room, and the name of his teacher. He looked at it, then at the school entrance, finally back at the card. His lips stretched slowly into a knowing smile. He carefully tore the card into two equal parts, then stuffed them into the pocket of his jeans. Balancing on the yellow line painted on the school grounds, he twisted around and then strode purposefully out of the yard.

Down the block Willy began to feel lightheaded, not really woozy, but nicely light, feeling good about playing hooky. He raised his face toward the sun, inhaling the morning, and began making his way to noplace.

His body felt loose and easy as he moved up and down the blocks, taking in the sights: people dodging traffic, teasing children playing, hard hats with their drills, drunks, fast ladies (wild women, his mother said), and always the number runners. It felt great to be out in the late spring morning air. It even felt better that he'd decided not to go back to the school, hoping ole Bertha wouldn't find out.

Hours later he found himself in a Spanish neighborhood. Small groups of people sat or stood before the shingled houses in bad need of paint or repair. Dogs, tails drooping, padded in and out. Men grasped beer cans as they clapped down dominoes or argued in their rapid language. Willy passed a hydrant gushing water into the gutter. His spirits rose as the circles spreading on the pavement told him of the simmering summer to come.

He liked the feel of the area, happy to see how everybody knew each other, talking and laughing while small children chased around. No one had noticed him; he didn't mind. He was like the invisible man. People seemed to respect you more when they didn't see you—that's for sure.

The sun had already reached its height and was beginning to descend when Willy started home. By the time he arrived at the Bowers' brownstone, his legs were tired and aching. The old man's aged, tobacco-toned fingers tugged away at weeds, cupping them easily in his palms.

"Hi, Mr. Bowers," he called out, waving.

"Hi there, young fella." Willy stopped, watching him pat the fresh earth around the greenery. Mr. Bowers was from the West Indies. Willy liked him from the first time he met him four years before. He liked his melodious voice; its up and down sound made him laugh. Sometimes, a giggle would burst from Willy, and the old man would look at him, cocking one of his thin, salty eyebrows as if he couldn't even catch on to his own jokes. Willy specially liked the stories of Mr. Bowers' childhood, like the Big Catch, the one the old man repeated most, how he and his pals would wade into the clear seawater capturing fish in huge nets. Other times he described how they climbed tall trees that stretched toward sun-filled skies, pulling off bunches of green bananas or grabbing at hairy coconuts they would crack open on a rock to suck the sweet milky water. Sometimes they were chased down a dirt road after snatching mangoes from old Mr. Matthews' yard, clutching them to thin chests as their bare feet made dusty smoke. Willy loved listening to the stories, even though he had heard them countless times. He delighted in the old man's descriptions of endless sunshine days in a place that never knew freezing cold. None of the dirty, messy snow he'd always hated, ducking snowballs, slipping and sliding, trying to keep his behind off the ground. It must have been wonderful to be born in a place that never had winter.

"Say, Willy, isn't it your birthday?" Mr. Bowers asked, glancing up from his squatting position.

9

Willy's mouth dropped open in surprise. He hadn't remembered his birthday. Why should Mr. Bowers remember? His birthday, yeah. All of fourteen and so tall his mother had to buy new jeans for him two weeks ago. So tall that he could pass for seventeen when just last year people thought he was eleven or twelve. Now it was harder. It was easier when they thought he was younger. It was only when he had to *say* something that they thought he was younger. Then they looked at him real strange, as if he wasn't making sense.

"Don't you remember, Willy?" the old man asked, interrupting. "We celebrated your last birthday right out there in the backyard." The memory of the scrapbook warmed Willy as he recalled the day.

"Yeah." He grinned, relaxing and pulling over a worn, old beach chair. Last year they'd sat under Mr. Bowers' big maple, the old man's wrinkled fingers stiffly turning pages filled with photographs of celebrities he used to know when he played bass—signed pictures of The Duke, The Count, and even Billie Holiday. Mr. Bowers had come from the islands to seek his fortune when he was young and played in some of the famous bands of the time. He had all their pictures.

". . . until," Mr. Bowers was saying, "Mrs. Bowers got mad because I wouldn't come inside and ended up feeding my supper to the cat. What a birthday!" He laughed with soundless short gasps of breath. He always called his own wife Mrs. Bowers, which had seemed strange to Willy at first. But after he had visited the Bowers' home, he somehow understood. Inside the house was dark—dank, heavy drapes keeping the sunlight from the rooms. The place was too small for all that furniture—fat chairs covered with velvet, the color of blood, with patterned tracks running all through the cloth. The whole place smelled like an abandoned building. The first time Willy'd gone inside, he'd felt if he chanced sitting on one of those chairs, he'd be swallowed up just like the ole whale swallowed Jonah. But it was really Mrs. Bowers herself that got to him, with her shiny round face, her watery eyes, and her wig—not like the good ones they sold at Abraham and Strauss, but the cheap ones you could buy off Korean street stalls, unhuman hair, looping down her ears like in the yellowed pictures he'd seen in the old scrapbook, even though he knew none of the pictures were of her.

Mrs. Bowers did not like him. Of that he was positive. Instead of speaking to him, she'd give him a short nod, like a pecking cock. And if she happened to be in the foggy living room, she'd sit there with her back arched as if her body was strapped in that position, fingers twisted in her lap. Other times she'd stare so hard that Willy had to shift from foot to foot to keep from running for the door.

Now, idly watching Mr. Bowers pack dirt solid around his plants, Willy yearned for another scrapbook session. He wanted to do it all again. And maybe he could even tell Mr. Bowers about what had happened in the schoolyard, how he made such a fool of himself with those kids. He just wanted to talk and tried to project his wish into the top of the old man's head, but nothing happened. Mr. Bowers was into his gardening stuff.

Giving up, he said, "See you, Mr. Bowers," and with a wave Willy moved on up the stone path to his brownstone, grateful that ole Bertha wasn't going to bust in all loaded down with cake and ice cream for a party that nobody ever came to. That was *over*, once and for all—that's for sure . . .

Willy sat in the twilight studying the long shadows of the blinds against the wall, dark shapes that matched his mood. The dull evening yawned before him as the shapes merged in the room. He was bored to death. He flipped through the TV guide. Nothing on the boob tube—as ole Bertha called it.

Suddenly noise broke into the basement living room, bouncing through the bars of the open window. Willy could see legs in fast jiggling motion, pushing and skipping in play. For a split second he wished he could be in their midst, a little kid again. When he was small, there were children to play with. It's just after he got bigger . . . Blocking the noise from his mind, he thought about the day. Even thinking about the fun he'd had playing hooky didn't make him feel better. His thoughts splintered off into nothing, and he sank deeper into boredom. Times like these he just hated being alive.

A black man with a thin mustache was on the television screen, talking casually with another man on a bar stool. The man reminded Willy of his father. The last time his father had been around was—that's right—another birthday just four or five years ago. He was the last person Willy had expected to see that night.

There had been a soft knock on his door. He had wanted to be alone, still angry over his mother's insistence on lighting the candles, though none of the neighbor kids had shown up. The door had opened, followed by silence, and Willy turned his head to see a form silhouetted against the hall light. He jumped up from his bed, frightened by the broad frame that blocked the doorway. The shadow moved slightly, and Willy recognized the face from the small yellowed photo his mother kept in a junk drawer— a photo he used to study when his mother wasn't around.

"Hi, Willy," the man said. "Just thought I'd take a look in on you. How you been, okay?"

He nodded uncertainly. "Yeah, I guess—"

Willy wondered if he should invite him in or something. But the man did not move from the open doorway. The hand was firmly on the knob. "Not giving your mother any trouble, I hope."

Willy shook his head.

Then suddenly, "Are you reading?"

Why had he asked him that? Willy scowled. What had ole Bertha told him?

"Well, I gotta run now," the man said without waiting for Willy to answer. "I'll see you around, okay?"

"Yeah."

And that was all. His father turned and closed the door behind him, shutting out the light, leaving Willy in the dark of the room.

The kids had moved down the street, and Willy was glad of it. Hunger pains churned loudly in his stomach. Where was ole Bertha, anyway? He went into the kitchen to look at the clock. Eight-thirty. Well, at least the birthday bit would be over soon. Finally, he heard the door open. His mother looked refreshed, smiling, which annoyed him even more.

"Where were you?" he demanded.

"I stopped at a movie." She took note of his face. "What's the matter with you?"

"Nothing," he grumbled.

"Did you eat anything?" He watched her pull the wide-brimmed hat from her head. It left a depressed circle around her short Afro.

"I didn't feel like boiling hot dogs." He scowled. "How come you didn't come straight from work?"

Her eyebrows arched. "I told you I went to see a movie. What's this cross-examination, anyway?" Then her mouth widened into a large smile. "That's right, it's your birthday," she sang out.

No. No. Please . . .

Foam sloshed over her hand as she pulled the lid off a beer can, white drops evaporating in the air. She started to slam the refrigerator door shut, but noticed something and swung it wide again. Willy felt uneasy.

"You drank up all the milk and didn't go for more? Honestly. I've asked you so many times to replace what you use. I leave you money for that purpose."

Something was happening. What? What?

"What are you grinning at?" Was he? The refrigerator door had blocked off the bottom part of her body as if she'd been sliced in half, and she was holding the beer can straight up like the torch of the Statue of Liberty. He felt the bubbling begin low and deep in his belly. Damn. Damn. He was going to laugh. There was no stopping it, and he knew he shouldn't laugh—like so many times before. He tried to cave in his stomach, to press his belly button back toward his spine, to push back the rolling mirth. But the crazy laughter tore from him, bouncing against the walls, mocking him, and tears ran down his face. He caught ole Bertha's look of surprise, followed by one of sadness.

He fled to his room and locked the door, his body heaving from the subsiding giggles. He leaned against the dresser to catch his breath. Then it was over. He hated the awful laughing. Never any warning, either. And yeah, just like everything else, supposed to grow out of that, too.

Willy dropped down on the bed and buried his head in his arms. The spasms had stopped. Flinging himself over on his back, he looked at the old Lakers banner he'd nailed up summers ago, the faded flag covering the hole the hammer had made. There was a shiny poster of Julius—the Doc—Erving, and one of Muhammad Ali—the greatest! Now all he does is roach commercials, talking like he had a bunch of bubblegum in his mouth or something. Willy's gaze moved across to his record collection piled in a milk crate. His mother said they were the only things he ever really took care of. Why not? They were *his*, and only his, although he seldom listened to them any more. They were all scratched up anyway from playing them so much. He stared at the ceiling, his eyes tracing the strange grotesque shapes forming there. Then the sands rose and sleep came without notice.

Ugly scratching sounds were pushing through the layers of sleep. Willy fought hard against insisting consciousness. He didn't want to wake up. The scraping got louder.

Whrrr! Whrrr! Plastic wheels rolling on concrete. Those damn kids again!

He sucked his teeth, pulled the pillow from beneath his head, and squashed it against his ears. When he realized it was the doorbell and not the bikes, he sat up. His stomach cramped. He'd fallen asleep without eating.

The bell rang again, and he heard the sound of his mother's slippers.

Who *is* that? Yeah, bet it's the ole Jehovah's Witnesses, only one's got the nerve to wake you up Sunday morning, knowing they gotta if you not in church. He climbed out of bed and went over to the door, opening it just wide enough to see a woman follow his mother into the living room.

He closed the door quietly and waited, anticipating. Her call came a few minutes later, "Willy! You awake? C'mon out here, will you? I want you to meet someone."

At first the woman looked white, which scared him. White people always meant some kind of trouble, trouble for somebody anyway. Landlords. Police. Teachers. Then he noticed the full curve of her pinkish mouth, her artificially stiffened hair, the caramel glaze of her cheeks.

"This is your Aunt Bessie, Willy," his mother announced. The woman gave him a full bear hug. A thick rose-petal odor escaped from between her breasts, and his stomach lurched sickly. The woman leaned back on her heels, appraising him. What a big man he was—and my, how time flies and all the rest of the dumb things grownups say.

He shot a look at his mother. Her eyes were half

16

closed, her lips pressed together. "Aunt Bessie is your father's sister," she informed him. "She had to attend a funeral at a church a couple of blocks away and recalled that we lived over here."

"Willy, you know I haven't seen you since you were a bitty baby in a stroller?" She kept looking at him. Her black dress was above her bony knees like she was coming from an all-night party, not a funeral. And she didn't look much like his father, either. Then his heart almost jumped right out of his chest. His father! She was his *father's* sister.

"Do you—do you live far from here?"

Her slanted eyes were puzzled, wondering. "No sugar, not far at all. You can catch the bus right there on the corner."

He saw his mother's head tilt in surprise. Then he heard her toneless offer of coffee and his aunt's high-pitched decline. She gathered herself together to leave as if she'd been there for a long time and happened to remember another appointment.

She planted a wet kiss on his face, covering his nostrils, cutting off his breath. "Now, Willy, you make sure you come to see your ole auntie, you hear?" she said before releasing him. She was almost to the door before she stopped, cackling as she turned. "How you gonna get there with no address, you tell me." She pulled a crumpled envelope from her bag, peered at it. "Oh yes, my Con Ed bill. This'll be just fine. Can't pay them this month, anyway. My address is right on there." She pointed. "Keep in touch, Bertha. Remember, we're family." Her eyebrows arched mischievously.

17

She looked back at Willy. "You sure enough look like Hunt, like he done spit you out, I swear." And the woman was gone.

Back in his room Willy sat very still on the edge of his bed. It wasn't until that very moment that he had realized how much he wanted to see his father again.

## 2

The public housing development stood bleak and towering against the pale, cloudless sky. Spray-painted names, numbers, and slogans decorated the rusted bricks. Inside the building Willy waited forever for the elevator to reach the first floor. Its heavy door noisily slid open, slamming with a loud clang behind him. He pushed the button marked sixteen. The elevator did not move; the door did not open.

The back of Willy's neck began to prickle. It's stuck! Then the doors opened, and a little girl, around six or seven, got on. She stretched up on tiptoes, pushing two buttons at the same time—a trick! When the car jerked upward, she turned to give Willy a wise, knowing grin, exposing a missing front tooth. The tooth she did have was so big he wondered if there would be enough room for another one. As the elevator shook upward, he noticed there was no thirteenth floor. Crazy. How could they make such a mistake, skipping a whole floor?

The sound of rock music behind the door marked 16B told him his aunt was home. Aunt Bessie showed no real surprise at seeing him, disappointing him a little. She led him through a small foyer into a messy living room. Pillows of every color and condition were strewn all over couches and chairs. A rag doll, topped with red woolen hair, was jackknifed in the corner of a chair. Willy noticed the empty coffee cups, the bent-up soda cans, and the TV tray filled with cigarette butts, all smoked down to their tarred filters.

Then he spotted the upright piano against one wall. Mr. Bowers had told him about pianos like this. They could actually play all by themselves, he'd explained. Willy walked hesitantly over to it, checking out his aunt from the corner of his eye. She motioned to the piano stool, and he eagerly pulled it out, sat, and ran his fingers over the keys. His aunt left the room and returned with a large frosted bottle of orange soda.

"Here's a glass, honey." He took it, grasping the neck of the bottle. Willy didn't much go for sodas, but he knew people expected kids to like the stuff. He closed his eyes as the burning seltzer made its way down his throat.

"So, you're Hunt's big son. Now ain't that some-thin' . . ." Her shrill voice went a pitch higher.

"You call him Hunt?"

"Sure, honey, 'cause that's his name, his nickname. We all called him Hunt. Don't you have one?" she asked.

"One what?"

"A nickname."

"Uh-uh." He shook his head.

"Well, we all had one, all us kids on the block. They used to call me Chooby," she informed him with pride.

"Choobbee," he repeated, grinning. "Sounds like a sneeze or something."

Her laugh was a screech. "Maybe so, but it was a groovy name in those days."

Those days, those days again . . . Everyone had good ole days but him. He turned to her, studying her face. He realized she was much older than he'd thought, closer to Mr. Bowers' age than his father's.

Right, his father. He remembered the reason he was there.

"Aunt Bessie . . ." he began, butterflies fluttering around in his stomach.

"Speak up, boy. Don't be shy," she said, not unkindly.

"Well . . . well, I think I want to see my father."

She didn't reply. His heart dropped. Maybe she didn't know where he was. Maybe Hunt didn't want anybody to know where he lived.

"Think? Mean you don't *know* whether you want to see him or not?"

"Yes, I do," he affirmed quickly. It wasn't going right . . . He shifted his attention back to the piano, not quite ready for her to answer since, then, there would no longer be much reason to stay, and he liked his Aunt Bessie.

"You play the piano?" Willy asked.

"Some, not much. Just takes up space—that's all. Got to dust it all the time," she replied, her mouth twisted. "Your father plays real good. Used to do quite a few gigs in his day, all right. But he always kept a real job," she added hastily. "Didn't play the fool the way those other so-called musicians do."

He should have known—a musician! Just like Mr. Bowers, except Mr. Bowers played bass.

"I don't rightly know where he is myself," his aunt said, as if Willy had just asked the question. "Keeps moving around . . ."

Willy felt let down. His eyes shifted toward the window, not knowing what more to say. Then he sensed her movement.

"Wait. I think maybe I do have a number. Just remembered. He gave it to me the last time he brought me some money. I was behind in my rent. Could have put my little behind right out in the street, I swear, Jesus!" Her eyes rolled up.

Boy, she was fast. Like a freakin' cat she disappeared through the foyer, then returned, hugging a small notebook against her thigh. She held up a book of matches. "It's on this. He wrote it on here." She gave him the notebook, then held the book of matches at arm's length, squinting farsightedly at it. "I'll call out the numbers, and you can write it in the notebook. I'll tear it out afterwards."

A new panic shot through him. Why can't she write it herself? What was he going to do now? But he took the book and opened it to a page with a column of three-digit numbers.

"Oh, don't worry about that none. That's my combinations for the week to give the numbers man. Would you believe? The woman across the hall hit two weeks ago. Never plays, mind you, but hits, just like that," she said in disgust, snapping her fingers. "And I'm the one who got her to play," poking her chest with her fingers. "Now she's got a brand-new color TV. Wouldn't have none if it weren't for me, don't you know." Her lips puckered. "My numbers man got arrested with his list of numbers right in his pocket. Don't know who's going to take over his run . . ."

Willy was only half listening, going through painful

changes. He was going to have to do it. He was going to have to write down the stupid telephone number. No way out. His aunt had stopped talking, regarding him with narrowed eyes.

He held the pencil between two fingers, pushing it, laboring with his usual scrawl, beginning to sweat. When he finished and looked up, it was right into her paled amber pupils.

"Yes," she murmured, "I can't write too good myself."

The heat was spreading through him.

"Never got past the third grade," she went on. "I was the oldest girl in the family, so I had to quit school to help my momma work in town. I still clean white folks' houses sometimes, when times get rough. Things ain't really changed much."

He wasn't quite sure what she meant, but he liked her to talk. He loved hearing about places and things people did. He could tell she was from the South, like Mr. Bowers was from the West Indies. But now she'd stopped talking altogether.

Willy shifted on the piano stool before he saw her eyes on him again. She frowned slightly, as if wondering who he was. Then she suddenly looked to a spot over his head.

"Now ain't that something. Time just keeps on a-running wild, like geese a-flying. I got company coming, and the place is a natural mess."

"I was thinking of going . . ."

"But you come back real soon, you hear?"

"Yes, ma'am."

23

"Ain't you the proper gentleman?" Her strawberry mouth spread wide. "Bet you didn't know your ole aunt's got a beau, did you?" Her bony shoulders made rhythm in the air as she spoke.

Willy shook his head.

"Well, I do," she cooed. "Met him right down there at Bohacks, buying all that dab-dab food. I knew he needed some good nourishin', I can tell you." She sprang up again, her sudden movements starting to bug him. "Gotta figure out my menu. How's about ribs, or chicken? Think he'll like that?"

"I guess so . . ."

"Me, too."

He submitted himself to the bear hug and the wet smothering kisses. He let himself out since she'd already gone into the kitchen and begun pulling out her pots.

Later, Willy leaned against the inside of a phone booth, thick hot air forcing him to slide open the door. His hands were so clammy from heat and nervousness that the receiver slipped from his grasp.

The phone rang four times before a tired female voice answered on the other end. "Yeah?"

"Is Mr. Harris Palmer there?" His voice sounded squeaky.

"Who is this?" The tone was harsh, suspicious.

"This is Willy."

"Oh, you're a feller . . ."

"Yes, ma'am," he replied, his forehead perspiring.

"Well, Hunt ain't here."

The soft lump hardened in his throat. "Do you know when he'll be back?"

"Nah, I don't keep no tabs on him."

"Can I leave a message?"

The woman sucked her teeth, disgusted. "Don't make me no never mind. Lemme get a pencil."

"No, it's all right. Just tell him to call me—Willy— during the day."

"Yeah, okay." There was a click, and the phone went dead.

Willy wondered vaguely about the clacking sound he heard until he realized it was his own body rocking against the booth door.

The days stretched long, following fitful nights of tossing wakefulness, ending in wide-eyed watchful orange dawns that faded slowly into midday's sun. Each time the phone would ring, Willy felt like he was about to jump out of his skin. One week followed another, merging, until the school term had ended, and summer began like a ball of fire. No call came from Hunt.

Then ole Bertha did her number, asking a whole bunch of questions, about his aunt, about the visit, about his health, getting next to his last nerve.

"It's just hot, that's all," he answered her.

"You're right about that," she countered. "Say, maybe we can get to the beach early this time, Sunday, maybe. We haven't gone for a couple of years."

"I can't do that . . ." he said peevishly.

"Why not?" she asked, surprised.

He watched a drop of sweat trickle down the side of her face. "Don't you know I'm too big to go around with you like that any more?" he responded sullenly.

"Well, I'll be—"

He left her standing there open-mouthed in the heat of the dimly lit room.

Later Willy realized that only three weeks had passed since his call. He heard from his father during that week. Outside his window the sky had turned blue purple, blocking out the earlier balmy feeling of summer's sun. Willy's head jerked up at the sound of the phone's ring. His mother called his name.

Damn. It was the wrong time. He'd told that woman to have his father call during the day. His legs turned to rubber as he walked toward his mother. The receiver was loose in her hand, and she stared at him. Was she angry? He couldn't tell . . .

His feet hugged the cool parquet squares, excitement building to such a point he didn't know whether he'd be able to talk. How should he greet him? What should he call him? Harris? Hunt? Dad—?

"This is Willy," he said simply.

"Yeah, I know. Got your message. Sorry I couldn't get back before. I was out of town." Right, thought Willy, understanding, probably on a gig. "So, how's it going?"

"Okay, okay—" Willy breathed into the mouth of the receiver.

"You're not in any trouble, are you?"

"Me? No. No . . ." Why did he ask him that?

"So, what's up?"

He pulled air into his nostrils. "Nothing. I just wondered if I could . . . maybe, see you sometime, you know . . ."

A long time seemed to pass. "I hear you. Yeah, that's a bet. Say, didn't you just have a birthday?"

What is this? Everybody's gotta go on about my birthday?

"Yes . . ."

"Getting to be a big man, huh?"

"I guess so . . ."

"Fourteen, right?"

"Yes."

"Sure, we can meet. Where?"

Oh boy—that's right, where? He sure can't come here. We could meet on the corner— No, that's no good. Where? Ideas seemed to jump in and out. Willy considered a few, discarded most. He was afraid Hunt would hang up. Then as if from nowhere he thought of the little boat, bobbing in some far corner of his memory. Another birthday, maybe? But how old could he have been when they'd gone to the lake to sail his new boat?

"I was thinking, maybe the park, near the lake? You know, right next to the boathouse. There're some benches out near the back."

"Great. How about this Friday, three o'clock?"

"Great." And it was done.

Willy replaced the receiver with great care, his lungs emptying. His relief was cut short by a sudden concern for his mother. She'd gone out of the room while he talked to his father. Anyway, what could she say? Why should she say anything? He had a right to see his father if he wanted to, but he couldn't get rid of a feeling of guilt during the next few days.

As suddenly as the morning heat had arrived that Friday, it dropped into a coolness that was like a fall afternoon. A lone cotton cloud stubbornly hung on in the steel blue of the sky. Willy half expected the leaves to turn brown and blow away in a gush of wind. For the umpteenth time he reviewed what they had discussed—the place and time.

It's okay, he tried to console himself as he sat on the bench, smiling at the glittering lake. This gave him more time to think, to figure out what they'd do. He didn't know why it took him so long to think about calling his father in the first place. Hunt would help him—that's for sure. Whatever was wrong he could make right. A warm feeling slid into him as he pictured himself walking down the street beside the big man he'd seen in the doorway. Maybe it was a good thing that he'd grown so tall in the last few months. They might even be the same height! Hunt. Yeah, he really dug his name, too. Sounded like a warrior or something, a hunter—a champion!

Maybe they'd end up going to eat, to a restaurant for some good ole grits. No, a Chinese restaurant is better, not those fast-food joints, but the one where they give you cloth napkins and serve you out of silver platters, like where he'd gone a few times with his mother. His father would sure enough go for that. Perhaps an Italian place. You get a lot of food in there, spaghetti for days! Hey! Maybe he wouldn't be hungry at all. Maybe they'll just do something together instead of feeding their faces. Bowling, now there's a real man's game. But what if he falls flat on his face, the way he did everything else? What would Hunt think about his idiot son then? Gotta forget about the bowling . . .

He heard the mournful cry of a hidden bird and looked around, but couldn't find it. Caw—caw— Then the call stopped.

It came to him with a sudden shock. His father was not going to show up! His mind threw up fast excuses. Hunt got sick. A special gig turned up. He mixed up the days. He's just late, that's all— Wait! Suppose he got mugged! In his mind's eye Willy saw the hoodlums spreading out behind his father. Stupid! Why had he said the park? Nobody goes into the park nowadays except for those crazy joggers.

Boy, it's really getting cold. He wrapped his arms about himself, his fingers touching the goose bumps. Who'd ever think the temperature would take a nosedive? One day so hot your feet is burning, the next you're almost sorry you didn't wear your snow boots.

His chest heaved. Someone was coming—coming, running. It was him. It *had* to be him. His eyes narrowed, straining, but the lowering sun was too bright against the moving form. Finally the shimmering outline of purple turned into a person. Willy saw it was a jogger—just a jogger.

He was a youngish white man, his blue eyes widening as he saw Willy, fear pouring into his face. He thinks I'm going to jump him, Willy realized with disgust as the purple shadow crossed over him. He wanted to yell after him,

"I'm just waiting for my father, stupid!" Instead, he kept watching until the streak became smaller and disappeared altogether at the edge of his vision.

The white sun was almost hidden with the coming dusk, and the park was still, an early mysterious luster settling over the silhouetted buildings, merging with the gray-green mass of bushes and trees. Willy listened to a church gong, mournful, sad. He thought of the hidden bird.

His legs were stiff as he made his way onto the dirt path leading out of the park, so that walking seemed hard and slow. People coming home from work hunched their bodies against the unexpected change of weather. Willy's steps quickened. Maybe he had called—

Ole Bertha was in the kitchen. She hadn't changed from her street clothes. Willy didn't remember seeing the lavender suit before, and he liked how it softened her look. She was really a good-looking woman, his mother, ole Bertha . . .

"Hi, Willy," she greeted him.

"Hi."

"Why aren't you wearing your sweater?"

"I didn't know it was going to get so cold."

"Well, it's not really cold, you know, just a little cool for this time of year."

So what? What difference does it make? It was cold *to him*. He knew he didn't have to ask. Hunt had not called. Then he noticed the smell in the room. His mother wore a silly grin, and he felt the slow anger growing inside him. So now she wanted to heap some ole greasy fried chicken on him. Stopped cooking any good food when she went on that health food kick—rabbit food for days. Now fried chicken supposed to make everything just fine. Great!

He watched quietly as the thin smoke circled her head, curling into an expanding halo, the acrid aroma making his nostrils quiver.

"It's burning," he told her dully.

His mother's head twisted sharply. Willy took advantage, rushing to his room. "Fried chicken—nicely burnt," he muttered aloud, bitterly. He slammed the lock closed.

All kind of jangled thoughts kept racing through his head. He felt tired, confused, sapped. Maybe Hunt didn't really want to see him. Maybe he didn't want to be bothered with his dumb son. But how could he know? His mother didn't even talk to him—at least Willy didn't think she did.

What should he do now? Try calling again? Maybe something really happened . . . What to do? What? What was he going to do for the summer? Yes, he wanted his father for the summer. Needed him to tell his problems. Needed to do things—go to the pool, to the ball games, get on the basketball court! He'd really show him how to play, pay back on those lousy kids messin' over him.

The sound of the phone ringing cut off his thought. It rang three times, each time the sound jarring, biting deeper into his brain. His mother laughed. Damn. Damn. Then the muffled sounds of her voice went up and down, giggling, and, finally, silence. Great, just what he wanted— no sound at all. He heard a far-off rumble.

Suddenly, a bolt of lightning exploded his whole room into bright daylight. For a split second he saw everything in detail, stark black and white like the old movies on TV. Again, the lightning cracked wide, ripping up the blackness. That's right, his heart raced. Do it! Do it! Rain! Pebbles of water smashed against the windowpane. His body arched, pushing to meet the next flash. Yes! Yes! If he was lucky, it would come right in on him and strike him dead!

He flung himself down and smothered his face in the striped blue bedcovers.

"Damn you, Hunt!" he shouted to the world. Sobs tore from his depths, the mattress rocking beneath him, keeping time.

3

The time lagged, days stretching into unending nights, but Willy's father never called back. Pain lay just beneath the surface of Willy's skin. Maybe he was sick. He wished he was, sick and maybe dying. That would be good. He could not rid himself of a feeling of lightness, as if he was dangling in space—nothing above or below him. Then ole Bertha, staring at him all the time, saying nothing.

Later the dull ache changed into a rushing anger, shooting through his head, bounding out, swirling around his room and through space until it reached behind the shadow of his father's face. He was frightened of the awful feelings he kept having, but he was mostly scared by the anger he'd begun to feel toward his mother. A new guilt seemed to eat at him. Then, now, this whole business about having meals together. Never had to do that before. Stupid, just plain stupid. And the food never tasted like nothing— even with stuff like meat loaf and baked potatoes, butter swimming on top or the ole fried chicken number. He would swallow big chunks, anxious to be finished and done so he could go back to his room. But even in his room he felt bad. The TV was nothing but the pits. He couldn't get into his favorite game of watching the picture with the volume off, trying to figure out what the people were saying. Worst of all, summer was starting without him.

Willy didn't know how many days had passed since he'd sat alone in the park. Felt like weeks, and he hardly remembered much. Later he found out only a few days were gone. One morning he opened his eyes to lemon sunlight peeping through the bedroom window. The whole room looked strangely beautiful. He knew something was different and sat up, wondering. His hands flew to his chest. The weight inside was gone. And he found that he could easily move his arms and legs. He must have been sick or something and was now better . . .

He listened for his mother's hurried preparations for work, but she'd already gone. That was all right, too. He swung his feet to the floor, a sense of expectancy propelling him into the bathroom. A cold dash into the shower and he was out, anxious to catch up—to what, he didn't know.

Minutes later Willy stood in the center of the kitchen, rubbing a towel across his back. It felt good. For the first time in days he was anxious to know what his mother had left him for breakfast. Usually, he had ended up by dumping the wheat cakes, cheese omelette, or other stuff into the garbage. Instead, he'd taken large gulps of milk from the gallon container, welcoming the icy shock to his body, but he hadn't been able to eat—that is, until now!

He was starving! He peeked under the covered platter. Banana fritters! He'd thought they'd gone out of style. Willy attacked with his fork, his hunger unreal. Within minutes he was into the kitchen closet, emptying a Wheaties box and pouring his mother's half-and-half into the bowl. In ten minutes he was out on the street.

Walking down the block, Willy was amazed at how bright and sparkling the trees looked, surprised at the newness of everything he saw. His spirits bounded as he stepped out to watch the day's opening. He passed storekeepers heaving up the accordionlike gates that had kept out night crime, surveyed the Korean little people with their ever-present grins hosing down vegetables and gleaming up their fruits. Stray dogs sniffed at food scraps, and workers darted crazily across the streets to catch buses. Willy felt all at one with the world.

Mr. Bowers was standing in front of his house when Willy returned. He couldn't believe his eyes! Instead of his usual overalls, Mr. Bowers was wearing a suit—a white suit, at that. The old man stood motionless, gazing high at the Brooklyn skyline. He looked like a statue in the bright morning sun.

Seeing Willy, he beckoned, knocking a stiff straw hat askew on his thinning gray head.

"What's happening, Mr. Bowers?"

"Nothing's happening, my boy . . ."

"Well, how come you all dressed up like that?"

Mr. Bowers grinned at him, his gold front tooth a jewel in the morning light. "Willy, you're a sight for sore eyes," he replied, ignoring the question.

"Me?" Willy thought to himself, wanting to laugh.

"I haven't seen you in a dog's age," the old man commented. "I thought you went away, maybe."

Willy dropped his eyes. "No—I just haven't been out much lately."

The elder man scrutinized him from behind his wire rims as they sauntered toward the back of the house. Willy trailed along behind him.

"Umm-humm," Mr. Bowers commented thoughtfully, looking up toward the sky. "Bet winter's going to be early this year. It hasn't been this cold in July since 1939. We once had Christmas in July, you know."

"No kidding," Willy replied, getting interested.

"Well, all the boys in the band had earned some good money in the downtown clubs that summer. We decided to go into Harlem and give presents out to poor children. One of the best times I ever had. Christmas in July," he repeated, pleased with the memory.

Willy conjured up the parade in his mind, a whole bunch of musicians in their tuxedos, in the bright heat of July, their instruments all piled in cars as they rode up and down Harlem streets giving out Christmas gifts. Great stuff!

The back door opened. With a quick glance, Willy caught a glimpse of pale violet airiness. His head jerked around and he saw the girl. She was almost as tall as Mr. Bowers, and she looked like him. His eyes grew wide.

"Oh, yes, Willy, I'd like you to meet my niece. Kathleen flew in from the islands. We just got back from the airport."

"Hello, Willy. I'm here on holiday," she said with a quick and open smile. Her voice had the same melodious sound as her uncle's, but different still, making Willy think of little tinkling bells.

36

He was engulfed by his usual shyness, but he managed to say, "Glad to meet you," a little too loudly. He leaned forward awkwardly to take her offered hand. The touch of her fingers was soft and cool, but as they tightened, he thought her grip kind of strong for a girl. She must be only a few years older, he guessed, maybe seventeen or eighteen. Her brow was high above deep-set, luminous eyes that reflected the violet shades of her dress. She had smooth sepia-toned skin darker than her uncle's. Her hair was plaited into two long braids, and with her high cheekbones, she looked just like an Indian.

"We're about to have some brunch," she announced pleasantly. "I do hope you will join us, Willy." She glided out into the yard to join her uncle already seated at his worktable. Behind her, Willy's weakened legs carried him unsteadily. Under a protecting tree, the table was covered with a shiny plastic flowered sheeting.

Willy dropped into a chair, wondering where Mrs. Bowers was. He looked curiously at the full bowls Kathleen had placed before them. She explained that codfish and boiled plantains were foods traditional to her homeland. She grasped the neck of a narrow bottle filled with a cloudy, reddish liquid flecked with tiny seeds.

"Now this," Kathleen informed Willy, her small chin jutting out, "this pepper sauce I made especially for Uncle, but . . ." she leaned forward confidentially, "you have to be careful how much you use, Willy. It is quite hot." She didn't have to worry about him none. He wasn't about to touch that stuff—it looked too nasty.

"And, dear boy, this is ginger beer." She held up another bottle from a picnic basket. It was brownish with no label. "It's almost as potent." She threw her head back and laughed merrily. Willy didn't catch it.

"Rubbish!" uttered Mr. Bowers, breaking his silence. "The drink is as mild as babe's milk."

But Willy didn't notice Kathleen's change of expression as he took the drink Mr. Bowers poured for him. Tears sprung quickly to Willy's eyes as he took a sip, and he almost sprang up himself—to run home for ice water. But he quelled the impulse. He had to sit and suffer. He wasn't gonna act the fool—that's for sure.

When he looked over to see Mr. Bowers' reaction, the old man was staring into space, one hand fingering the gray bristle on his chin.

Kathleen glanced at him. "I'm sure Auntie's operation will be successful, Uncle."

Willy was surprised; that must be why she wasn't out here eating with them. He hadn't known Mrs. Bowers was sick. "She'll be in and out of the hospital in a jiffy, God willing," Kathleen offered gently.

Sounded strange for a girl to say something like that. Willy had only heard that expression from older people— church people.

As the old man and the young girl continued talking to each other, Willy tasted the food, silently cursing the huge breakfast he'd polished off earlier. He found the fish stringy, forcing him to chew for a long time before he could swallow, but it tasted real good. Beginning to feel more at ease, he leaned back in the picnic chair. He realized from their talk that Mrs. Bowers had been ailing for some time. Kathleen would be taking care of the house and preparing her uncle's meals until Mrs. Bowers recovered. She was so young when she'd visited the States last that she was hoping to get around and see the sights, like a tourist, she'd added. So she was here for two reasons.

As the two continued to talk about family and friends "from home," Willy watched as her face broke into a sudden smile. Sometimes her body would swing to the side as she laughed at Mr. Bowers' corny jokes. After a while the old man leaned back in his chair, his legs sprawled, and looked out through half-closed eyes.

"So tell me about Mavis, child . . ." he murmured.

Kathleen, who had a paper cup to her mouth, almost choked with laughter. "Aunt Mavis has seven children, fifteen grandchildren, and she's as big as a house!" Her arms opened wide, indicating the size.

"Nonsense!" Mr. Bowers uttered with mock disbelief.

"Worse than that, Uncle. She's so huge that her grandsons had to make a special wicker chair for her to fit in." She was laughing so hard that her beautiful eyes began to tear at the corners, and the grass got a dose of ginger beer.

But Willy noticed the cheerfulness had vanished from Mr. Bowers' face, and his eyes were misty. "She was such a pretty little thing—"

The girl's laughter ceased abruptly. "Oh, Uncle, I'm sorry, I forgot—"

Willy had never seen Mr. Bowers' face so gentle, so young-looking. "Ah, my child, that was almost forty years ago . . ."

Mr. Bowers pulled himself up laboriously, pouring himself more ginger beer and offering the bottle to Willy.

Willy shook his head. He was picturing Mr. Bowers as a young man, courting this "pretty little thing," maybe with flowers in one hand, candy in another, like in the old-fashioned Hollywood flicks he watched on TV. People seemed nicer then . . .

But something really bad must have happened back then with Mr. Bowers. Maybe Miss Mavis had another boyfriend and turned him down. Would sure enough explain why he'd ended up with someone like ole ugly Mrs. Bowers.

The pleasant lightness of the morning had disappeared into breezeless air. Kathleen concentrated on cleaning the table as Mr. Bowers remained in the past, his narrow legs sprawled in front of him and his white suit rumpled. Maybe he should help her clear the table, but she was just about finished. He pulled himself to his feet. "Well, I guess I should be getting back now. I really had a nice time."

"Oh, Willy, you're not going already?" Her eyes met his over her uncle's bowed head. "Maybe I'll walk with you."

They walked slowly next door to Willy's house, taking the path between two rows of tiny white pebbles. He halted at his front steps. For some reason he did not want her to know he lived on the basement level.

"What a nice house," she commented. Willy shot a look at her, then at the house. There was no real difference between the two houses except for a different paint job. "Uncle tells me they're called brownstones. They're not really made of brown stones, are they?" she asked.

Willy had never thought much about it. "I—I don't think so . . ." He kicked at a half-pint whiskey bottle on the gravel, hoping she wouldn't ask anything else he knew nothing about. He tried to think of something to say. His eyes caught the row of bushes enclosing Mr. Bowers' front garden. "We can't grow flowers in our yard. It's cemented." Then he added quickly, "Not by us, by the owner."

"Oh, it's not your house?"

Willy felt the heat rise in his face. "No—"

"Uncle had a tenant too one time," she went on. "He says people have such a hard time finding a place to live nowadays that he'll probably rent out again."

Willy was thinking hard. He didn't see why Mr. Bowers should care. People living with you always meant trouble. He was glad when the tenants over him upstairs had moved out. All that noise. Stereo blasting all night long. All the fighting . . .

Kathleen crossed her arms over her chest. "I guess I should go back. See you tomorrow?"

He wasn't sure whether she was asking a question or not.

"Yeah, sure . . . okay."

Willy watched her climb over the small picket fence that divided the property. Just like a boy—no, not exactly, smoother, more graceful, like the deer Bambi.

Maybe she doesn't really want to see me tomorrow like she said. Some people say things because they think you expect them to. Yet . . . she didn't seem like that.

The next morning Willy perched on a chair in front of the barred basement living room window, waiting. Maybe it would have been better if Mr. Bowers' niece had been a boy. Would make things a whole lot easier, that's for sure. They could do "boy" kind of things, ball games, stuff like that. They could play basketball. Beat the pants off the guys in the schoolyard. He never got along with girls, though; if boys were bad, girls were worse. Giggling all over the place. Covering their mouths, laughter spilling out, always over something dumb. But Kathleen wasn't like them at all. Maybe it's because she's older. . . . Maybe because she came from the West Indies . . .

It wasn't until the afternoon sun had inched over the rows of dim-colored houses that Willy ventured out. He had waited, and she hadn't shown up. He'd just have to go to her. But he shouldn't. People shouldn't say what they don't mean, he thought resentfully. If she didn't mean to come, she shouldn't have said so. He should stay right where he was. But, wearied of indecision, he decided to go over to the Bowers'.

Willy had hoped to find Kathleen alone, but he heard voices coming from the back of the house. Kathleen was sitting with Mrs. Bowers under a shaded vine. The girl's back was toward him, so it was the woman who saw him first, her watery eyes filling as he approached. Should go back home, but it was already too late. The woman's stare held him rooted.

Kathleen sensed his presence. As she jumped up, the crocheting she was working on fell from her lap.

"Hee—loo! I didn't know you were here, Willy."

"Pick up your work, girl," the woman said tonelessly. "You've soiled it."

Kathleen bent to retrieve the piece, exposing the top of her head. A straight pale line parted her hair down the middle.

"Are you looking for Uncle? He had to go to the bank this morning. He'll be back soon."

He stood there before the two of them, feeling ridiculous. He lifted a shaking index finger, pointing. "I'm sorry. I didn't mean for you to dirty it."

"Oh, this old thing," she scoffed. "Not to worry, I make plenty of them. Just to pass the time." She'd left the chair and was standing close to him. He was overcome with confusion.

"Guess what?"

"Wh—what?"

"I am glad you came. I'd like you to accompany me to get some ice cream. You know, the kind they make here, all soft and creamy."

"Oh, yeah. I know the kind you mean. They sell it at Carvel's. Just a few blocks from here." He pointed.

"Good. Let's go."

She gave her aunt a slight nod. Kathleen grabbed his hand and pulled him along. Willy felt as if he were floating.

Near the gate, he glanced back over his shoulder at the woman. She was sitting in the same position, straight-backed, her huge bosom pushed against the navy-blue silk of her dress, her face flat, expressionless.

———

43

Willy was conscious of the girl's height as they walked together down the city block. Tall as she was, he was still taller. He now had reason to be glad about how fast he'd grown. A warm, satisfied feeling settled into him as they strolled. It seemed to Willy that people were looking at him with new respect. Then they turned the corner, and he saw the long line in front of the store. It would take forever. Forget it!

They stood, stuck in one spot for what seemed almost an hour. From the line, gloomy, sweaty faces stared back at him. What were they looking at? Were they sizing him up? Maybe they're wondering what she was doing with *him*. He forced his eyes away, trying to focus on the window cleaner working feverishly on a store window across the street.

Suddenly his heart began to pound. His fingers searched frantically through his pockets, but he already knew, remembering the exact number of coins that were supposed to be in the bottom of his pocket. But he found nothing. He'd forgotten to pick up the money! Stupid! Stupid! Sweat sprang out on his forehead as panic poured through him.

The minutes crowded in on him. What to do! Maybe just explain that he forgot his money? What good would that do? The line was moving faster. He wanted to cry.

"Willy . . ." Kathleen was leaning toward him. "Willy, I hope you don't mind, but I'd like to treat you. I am just so happy to be here, and besides, Uncle gave me this." He saw a crumpled five-dollar bill in her hand. He was struck with a feeling of relief mixed with shame.

"What flavor do you want?" he asked, his voice low, quavering.

"Strawberry," she announced brightly. She beamed as she took the dripping cone. "Next time," he said, too loudly, "I'm treating."

After they finished their cones, neither wanted to rush back. Willy couldn't believe that everything had turned out all right at Carvel's. Kathleen acting like nothing happened made him feel at ease with her, more comfortable than he'd ever been with anyone else before. As they walked idly, the weather began to change, the clouds thickening and darkening above.

"I think it's going to rain. Maybe we should turn back," Willy said.

She looked over at him, a little surprised. "Why? Won't it be over soon?"

"Could be, but we shouldn't take any chances."

She followed his gaze, squinting into the sky. "It does look rather ominous, doesn't it . . . ?"

They got caught in a thunderless storm. The rain crashed down in torrents as people ran helter-skelter for cover, rivers of water swelling and cascading over clogged drainpipes. Willy's sneakers were instantly flooded. They sloshed and squeaked as he trotted behind the girl, who seemed to be having a great time. Willy watched as she ran backwards, laughing. She's crazy, he thought happily, feeling wonderful.

Finally they took shelter in a doorway, thoroughly soaked. Willy saw the amusement on her face as she watched others dashing from the deluge. Holding her dress at the edges, she flopped the water from her skirt. The damp fabric clung to her slender body, and he suddenly felt flustered. He could see almost right through to her skin. He forced his eyes away, embarrassed.

"We have such rain back home," she was saying, "coming down hard like this, but only for a few moments." The doorway was narrow, such a tight fit that Willy was acutely conscious of her closeness. The sweet damp fragrance rose from her body, wafting through his nostrils into his head.

Willy felt strange confusion at the confinement; his heart fluttered unevenly. The rough edge of wall behind him scraped against his back, but he dared not move. Then he spotted a man running in their direction, shirt slapping behind him. They pushed apart to give him room. The man pulled out a wrinkled tissue and wiped his face.

"Ain't this some shit?" Willy's eyes darted to the girl, but she appeared not to have heard. "I was on that damn bus, too," the man went on. "Should have kept my black butt right on it." Then Willy saw Kathleen flash a look of disapproval at the intruder, her eyes deepening. There was no more talk among the three crammed silently together in the space until the rain stopped.

Perhaps it was the storm that disrupted the mood, maybe it was the man invading their private space, but a shyness settled between them. The sun remained tucked behind the hanging clouds, its weak light emphasizing the grime on the houses, the piled-up garbage, and the dismal decay of the neighborhood.

They walked wordlessly to her house. "So, will I see you tomorrow?" A question this time. Now he could decide.

"Sure." The corners of his lips turned up. "Think you'd like to go to the movies?" Where did that come from?

"Why not? That would be quite nice."

The next day they met on the corner, as agreed, and went to the only neighborhood theater that hadn't been turned into a church. The movie was one of those horror films that Willy hated—like how the music came in at the beginning with mournful violins, setting up the mood. The two slid into their seats, and Willy sat suffering through the whole lousy picture.

He welcomed the abrupt ending as a bodiless bloodied head came on the screen. The girl stiffened in the darkness, her hand grabbing his arm. "Oh, my goodness! How awful!" As her hand relaxed, lifting, he immediately missed its pressure.

The lights came on, and Willy was startled to see Kathleen still seated, a grin on her face. "Let's see some of it again, Willy."

Oh, for goodness' sake—"But, Kathleen," he protested.

"Oh, don't be a spoilsport, Willy. It's so nice and scary," she added, wriggling her body.

He stood there in front of his chair, uncertain. A chubby boy tried to pass him to get to the aisle. He decided to go out, but turned to Kathleen. "Want some popcorn?"

"I'd love some, Willy."

As he walked grudgingly to the candy counter, he wondered vaguely if they showed horror movies and sold popcorn in the place where she came from. Maybe they didn't. Maybe that's why this second time around.

As they passed the greasy carton back and forth, Willy learned that Mrs. Bowers was going to the hospital the next morning. And he was glad, glad the old biddy would be away for a while. He shouldn't feel that way—he knew that—but the woman was spooky—as bad as this ole spooky picture. He stretched back as the music got louder, then sank deep into the cushioned seat.

During the next few weeks, they continued to see each other. Willy enjoyed their daily meetings. At first he hadn't given them much thought, sure that at some time she'd lose interest. Why did she bother with him in the first place? Wasn't he young and dumb? Could hardly read or write. Putting me in a class for stupid kids . . . Yet, she treated him like any other guy—went out with him, like a date. So, was she his girl? He couldn't stop thinking about her, so he probably loved her—like a girlfriend. But she might be thinking of him like a little brother. Maybe she had a younger brother and they went places together, and she pretended Willy was him . . .

But Kathleen felt like his girl, *to him*, and that's the way he was going to look at it. He was going to keep it that way. And—maybe she *was* his girl. Who's to say?

When they had gone to all the movie houses within a three-mile radius, they visited the botanical gardens and the museum next door. He'd hated the idea of the museum at first, remembering how it was when he was a little boy.

He always got tired and cranky and started crying, and his mother would scold him for not behaving. But going with Kathleen was another whole thing. He liked best checking the Egyptian room with its mummies and coffins. Of course she liked the room because it was spooky.

One morning as they walked past a storefront church, a rich baritone voice spilled out into the street from a loud-speaker—telling of sin, Sweet Jesus, and sprinkled with ah-mens. Kathleen wanted to go inside, but Willy hung back, knowing those holy roller people didn't like strangers bustin' in off the street. Besides, he didn't want to admit he was kind of leery about watching people "gettin' the spirit" and falling out screaming and carrying on so crazy. But Kathleen was really something! She didn't seem to care where she went. Lately he'd been feeling confident, more sure of himself, and he decided to take a stand. "C'mon." His voice was firm. "Let's get out of here." It worked. She fell into step beside him, and Willy's chest inched out a little.

The next day began with a fiery sun rising in the east, and the heat was on again. When they met for the day, Kathleen was wearing a white printed floral dress of sheer fabric that hung loose to her ankles. She said, "Uncle suggests rowboating. He was surprised that we'd been in the park so often and hadn't thought of going boating. In the summer everybody likes to go rowing."

The old fart. Had to interfere. "What's the matter, Willy? Don't you like the idea?"

"Sure, it's okay—"

"We don't have to—"

"No, it's okay—"

He should have known things were going too good to be true. Rowboating, would you believe? Especially since he'd never rowed in his life. It wasn't until they neared the boathouse that he realized it was near the place he was supposed to have met his father.

"I love to row," Kathleen informed him as she stepped into the boat he held steady. She grabbed the oars deftly, turning them inside her palms, getting their feel. "Come on, Willy. What are you waiting for? Get in." He placed one foot in gingerly, and the boat lurched wildly, leaving his other foot on the grassy mound. Damn. Damn.

"Put your foot in, hurry!" Kathleen exclaimed, and he managed to get his other foot in the boat, only to plop down on the burning aluminum. Oh hell—but he succeeded in burying a yell. She must have some tough behind to sit there like the seat ain't on fire. He wished he could be anyplace else in the world but in this damn boat—

In spite of his discomfort, he watched her with admiration. She rowed with the ease of a pro, laughing and giggling. "I do love it, Willy," she said, pulling hard on the oars. "I hope you don't mind too much," she said, breathing easily. "You can take the oars when we get to the other side if you want." Well, he was going to have to figure out how to duck that one since he wasn't about to try nothing new.

There were lots of people in the park, as if it were Sunday. Kathleen steered the boat toward the middle of the lake, the burning sun beating down on their heads. She rowed toward the edge of the lake where branches of a weeping willow leaned over to give them shade. The skirt of her dress had bunched up over her slender legs. Willy pulled his eyes away.

"So, what do you have to say?" Kathleen suddenly asked.

"About what?"

"Anything."

"Well, I don't talk much—"

"So I've noticed," her eyebrow arching significantly. For a split second he disliked her. "If my mother were here," she explained, "she'd probably say I had enough words for all three of us." She snickered. He tried to imagine her mother sitting in the boat, but all he could picture was Mr. Bowers' fat Mavis on the other side about to sink them.

"Tell me, Willy, why didn't you want to go rowing?"

"I told you it was okay—"

"No, I think not. I'm getting to know you. Something is wrong."

Willy thought for a while. "Well, I don't know how to row a boat. Besides," he hastened to add, "one time I was supposed to meet my father near here. He decided not to show up."

They turned at the sound of voices and saw another boat with a young couple and two small children, one leaning over the side, his small pudgy fingers splashing the water gleefully.

"We'd better take the boat back or they'll keep our deposit," Willy told her. Once the boat was returned, they walked along the edge of the lake.

"Willy, I know what you're going through. My father

lives in a big government house on top of a hill." She drew herself together as if she were cold. "He lives in that big house with his other children. They were born after us, after myself and my brothers and sisters." Her eyes seemed to lose their sparkle. "My mother is not married to my father. They refer to us as 'outside children.' "

They stopped beside a bench that had only three slats, but sat down anyway. "I suppose he is a good man. He is highly respected and such, supports us . . ."

"He visit you?"

"Yes."

"Well, you should be glad about that."

"I don't know . . . He always acts as if he's doing us such a big favor, as if it was a solemn duty he had to perform. And do you know, my mother still serves him tea on her best china." She looked at him, then away again.

Willy was confused. Her father took care of them, came to see them. What's the big deal?

"At least you know him," he commented.

"Yes, but imagine if I didn't. Then I could believe that he would be with us if he could, but fate somehow prevents him from doing so. I could imagine all the lovely things we would do together. But I can never forget that he prefers to be with his other family on top of the hill. His visits simply make it worse.

"But there he would be, self-righteous, with his suit and tie, sipping his tea and looking at his watch." She leaned against the back of the bench. "But I am happy enough." Suddenly she perked up. "I am fortunate to have good friends, and life is not really unpleasant back home.

The economy is a problem, but we do have a small farm to grow our food, some chickens, pigs—"

"They call them haawwgs down south," he interjected, wanting to show off.

"Oh, you've been south?"

"Me? Naw. It's just that one time some kids came to the house with their mother, and that's how they talked. Haawwgs, daawgs, haawwg-maaww." He laughed hard. "And I really liked them. I bet if there were more kids like them around, I would have friends."

Her eyebrows rose in dual arcs. "Willy, you're not trying to tell me you don't have friends, are you?"

There was the pressure, at the center of his forehead.

"Well, it's not my fault!" he burst out.

"Who's talking about anyone's fault, Willy?" She smiled. "I think you're shy, too, just like me."

Disbelief ran through him. Yeah, like who's fooling who? ". . . And I don't understand a lotta things people say, either. And me, too. I say things that people can't understand because I don't say them right."

A puzzled frown appeared on her face. "I understand you, Willy. What are you talking about?"

All at once he didn't care whether she understood or not. He was more concerned with what was happening inside him. Maybe she was asking too many questions. Maybe she was just talking too much, but suddenly he felt a force rising, building.

"I'm a dumb kid. Can't you understand!" he shouted at her, his words tumbling out fast. "And I know how to read! I know how to write. I can! And I can count, too," he lied shamelessly. "I know how to do a lotta things!" His hot breath hit the steaming air.

Her eyes were fastened on his face, her lips becoming a small oval as her finger raised to silence him. But the dam had burst, and his insides were rushing out.

"People always trying to cheat you in the stores, like you can't add nothing—looking at you like you just came off Mars. Kids calling you names all the time. I hate them! I hate all of them!"

He was on his feet swaying, breathing in hard, furious puffs through his nose. "Retarded!" he spat out, the pain roaring. "That's what I am!"

Inside his sneakers his feet felt swollen. He knew he couldn't fight back the tears, but he had to fight the pain in his feet, had to make them move. His body lurched, propelling him toward the exit of the park. He plunged into a thickening red mist, smashed into unseen people. Branches scraped his arm. Damn. Damn. He thought a voice called his name from far off. He couldn't be sure, and he could not see through the ruby haze. Then she took his hand.

Outside the park, a narrow space opened between them, allowing the park-side strollers to pass between. They stopped at the corner to wait for the lights to change. As they began to cross, a blue Toyota sped around the corner, cutting them off. He snapped to, his arms shooting across the middle of her body.

"Crazy! Want to kill somebody!" he yelled at the disappearing car. "They'll run right over you if you let them," he told her angrily, not looking at her, the shame of his actions still with him.

They stopped at a candy store not far from where they lived. As they made their way to the back, Willy saw there were only two stools left at the counter among aluminum poles standing pointlessly without seats. The store owner remained in the front, his eyes glued to a nine-inch portable television.

Willy studied the girl's face reflected on the food-speckled mirror opposite. "Willy, I think I can help you, really."

What? What now?

"I used to earn money teaching small children back home. I'm practically a teacher, really. I don't think anything is wrong with you, Willy. You can think. You can reason. You probably have some learning problems that can be overcome with extra tutoring."

The man finally dragged himself away from the baseball game, muttering. "Dumb bastard wouldn't know a strike if he saw one. Oughtta buy some fuckin' eyeglasses." Willy noticed the hand he placed on the counter had hair sprouting from its back like a soft bird's nest.

"What y'all want?" They ordered Cokes. He returned with two clouded glasses, plunking them down on the counter. "Ain't got no ice," he said, his voice gruff. "Still want 'em?"

Kathleen nodded, although she looked suspiciously at the unwashed glasses. "Just give us straws. We'll drink them out of the cans," she told the man.

A tutor? A teacher? He didn't like it. He didn't like

it one little bit. It meant everything would be different. He'd felt bad about what happened in the park, had hoped to make it up. But everything was changing. He wanted things to stay as they were. Like how they'd been dating and stuff. Why had he gone running off at the mouth? Now she wanted to have a go at him, too.

From the corner of his eye he saw her fumbling in her bag, taking out a small pad. "We'll need some things. Some books, pencils. We'll have to plan . . ." She backed off from the counter, beaming at him. "Oh, Willy, it's going to be fun—you'll see."

His hand wrapped around the warm tin. Willy felt sick as the hated burning seltzer hit the bottom of his belly, and part of the day splintered in the silence of his protest.

How would she be his girl now?

In the beginning, operations were set up in the Bowers' living room, but the old man kept up such a-coming and a-going flow that it appeared the two of them were inside the house just for the old man's personal pleasure. He would come in with his slippers dragging and drop questions like, "How are things going, youngsters?" or "What you folks working on today?" Then he'd settle himself in his stuffed chair, awaiting a full recitation, or worse, he'd barge in just as Willy was about to read aloud, to stumble painfully with the words.

Willy had hoped the old man had finally got the message that he should get out of their way when he took to staying in his room when Willy came. But Mr. Bowers had simply extended his reach. He'd call out to his niece for a "nice cup of tea, my dear," even hot chocolate, which Willy couldn't understand for the life of him. All that hot stuff in the middle of the hot summer. Crazy!

The idea came as Willy sat by himself, the math book on his knees as he stared at the meaningless pages. Kathleen bustled around making toast and coffee in the kitchen, not forgetting a "couple of cheese cubes on the side for her uncle."

"What about over my place?" Willy suggested when she came back. "My mother's at work all day. That way we could have privacy."

Kathleen laughed, teasing him, knocking him playfully on his arm. "Say, why do we need privacy? Got some thought I don't know about?" But she said she was feeling generous and he could have his way. If he wanted them to meet at his house, it was okay.

The second week Kathleen presented Willy with a spiral-bound notebook since his old loose-leaf book with its plastic cover was all marked up and had torn pages. This whole business actually began to work out better than he'd thought, and slowly he adjusted to the new arrangement. But Willy knew good and well that nothing stayed peaceful for long.

One late afternoon, as the energy-sapping heat mercifully began to leave the city, the questions started. Kathleen smiled up at him from a curled position in the corner of the couch.

"What kind of things do you like, Willy?"

He looked back quizzically. "What do you mean?"

"You know, like what do you like to look at on television?"

A drag. A real drag. "Mostly sports, I guess . . ." What he had really intended to do was surprise her with the vocabulary list he'd made up on his own—now, questions . . .

"Today, I saw a book I'd like to buy for you," she said.

He slumped against the back of the chair. "Look,

Kathleen, I don't see why you have to buy me things. You got me the notebook and the dictionary."

"It's part of the position," she responded, with her usual airiness. "Besides," she added, sitting forward, "Uncle gives me money. What am I supposed to do with it?"

"Use it on yourself. I have money, too," he insisted. "I can pay for my own stuff . . ."

Her eyes darkened. "I want to give you a present, Willy," she said softly. "If you can give, you should learn to receive as well."

Damn. Now, he had to get a lecture.

"Well, don't get me no books on sports—that's all," his bottom lip poking out.

"Why?"

"Because they're too hard to read, and there's a whole bunch of rules and stuff I already know about anyway."

The girl's shoulders jerked decisively. "Sports are out, then. We'll just have to make another selection."

We? She meant *her*.

He was relieved when he saw her straighten her legs, although he'd decided that he wasn't going to show her his word list. Serves her right.

The next day when Kathleen placed the blue-covered book on the end table, he muttered his thanks, then fumbled for his assignment. After she left for the day, he ran his fingers over the book's textured cover, pausing momentarily before carrying it back to his room. He purposefully tossed it on the foot of the bed and began to play around with the tiny calculator he'd bought with his own money.

An hour passed before he picked up the book to flip

through. He gave his pillow a punch before sinking back into its softness. The book balanced on his knees, he read the title aloud, struggling with each word. *"Kwami: A Boy from West Africa."* The book opened to a bunch of children carrying large baskets on their heads. Babies swung inside a cloth from the backs of their mothers. Everybody was smiling, smiling . . . And the colors, they were so bright, almost bursting from the slick pages. And there was Kwami himself on a big center page with his father. They were doing chores together. Funny how he had hardly never seen kids working along with their fathers over here.

He wanted to understand exactly what was happening and went searching for the paperback dictionary Kathleen had given him, locating it finally in the bottom drawer under his pajamas.

Later, much later, and slowly, the words began to string together. Willy realized that the boy was preparing for some important event. He had to read the page several times before he understood that the big occasion was the boy's step into manhood. Willy's eyes moved rapidly, sliding over sentences as he struggled, fighting his frustration until he reached Kwami's success. In the end, Kwami had passed all the tests. Willy felt really happy for him. But, his satisfaction was overshadowed by another thought. Yeah, maybe that was okay for Kwami in Africa, but what about him? What about Willy right here in Brooklyn?

Kathleen's second gift, another book, came a week later. It was more difficult—no pictures, for one thing. How was he going to figure out what's happening?

There were rows and rows of words. He would recognize one word, then run across a whole bunch that he didn't know. It meant grabbing the dictionary, flipping through for almost every word—and even then he couldn't figure out the definition. Many times he just wanted to throw up his hands, to give up. But something inside made him go on, a new purposefulness, a deep need to break through. Then, he discovered a method. He called a word out loud, to see if he could hear its meaning from the sound. Sometimes it worked. After a while the story became clearer. He eventually discovered that it took place in a ghetto, like Bed-Stuy, but this time in Chicago. Willy remembered from somewhere that Chicago was supposed to be a windy city.

Cal was the leader of a gang. He was a boy-man, the kind who would stop to pet the straggly head of a homeless dog or pour milk in a saucer for the cat who waited on the cracked step for him each morning. But Cal could be mean—like people who got in his way could get hurt. He also lived with his mother who seemed to have a lot of boyfriends. What a drag . . . his own mother. He was sure enough glad that ole Bertha didn't do that kind of thing.

One night when Cal's mother went out, he was left by himself, and she never came back. Wow! Ain't that something! For a long time Cal didn't know whether she was dead or alive. After a while he didn't care, and he learned how to take care of himself.

It took a long time for Willy to finish, and he didn't understand the last scene, it was so weird. Cal got dressed, brushed his hair, winked at himself in the mirror, then went to meet a stranger who wanted him to deliver a package. Cal seemed to be so happy about delivering this package—so crazy. Anyway, why would Kathleen give him a book like this to read anyhow? It wasn't good, like *Kwami*.

"Did you read it yourself?" he asked her.

"No, I was just browsing and looked through it and thought you'd like the story, Morning Glory." She poked him playfully in the stomach with her index finger, and he pulled away, unsmiling—

"What's the matter?"

"Well, are you supposed to like a book like that?" he asked. "Oh, I don't know. Maybe so, maybe not."

She dropped wearily on the couch.

"You look tired," he said, concerned.

"I look the way I feel. My aunt took a turn for the worse. We were at the hospital half of the night."

Mrs. Bowers! He'd completely forgotten about her. "Uh—how's she doing?"

"We called the hospital this morning, and they say she's doing as well as can be expected."

As much as he tried, Willy just couldn't muster any sympathy for the woman, worried only about what would happen when she came home. The thought made him shudder inwardly. Mrs. Bowers made him think of the darkness.

Kathleen was fanning herself with her hand.

"I'll be right back." He disappeared into the kitchen, returning with a tray of English biscuits that he'd gone all the way downtown to find. Boy, was she going to be surprised!

At first he thought Kathleen was reading, then saw she'd fallen asleep. Must have had a hard time last night, he thought as he sat down on the floor. The coolness of the wood felt good on his buttocks. He sat there, watching her still face. A light film of moisture coated her nose, gathering into little tiny beads at its tip. Her mouth was slack, and suddenly he realized from the way her face was twitching that she must be having a dream. He loved the way it felt, looking at her in secret, imagining himself in her dream world.

All at once, he had a crazy urge to touch her eyelids, to touch them with his lips. He noticed a slight stream of spittle at the corner of her mouth, and she moved, stretching her legs out the length of the couch. He grinned. Now she probably thinks she's at home in her own bed.

Her dress had gathered up above the smoothness of her thighs, exposing the edge of her panties. The color struck him: pale blue with a white lace border. Suddenly Willy felt an awakening in the center of his body, reminding him strangely of when they'd been caught in the rain and stood huddled up so tight. But there was something different happening this time, a hardness growing. He was so stunned that both his hands shot down, pushing hard against his crotch. It had only happened before when he'd been sleeping or in the morning, never just from looking . . . He shoved himself back, the force of his movement flattening him. He lay on the floor panting, sweat trickling into his eyes. He wanted her . . . He felt as if he wanted to push his whole self against her—this girl, helpless against his terrible thoughts.

Kathleen's eyes opened. "Oh, Willy—" She sat up. The tips of her fingers rubbed across her lips. "My goodness, isn't that something? I was really gone . . ."

He bent his left leg, hoping desperately she couldn't see what was happening to him. "I'm sorry, Willy—I just don't think we can have much of a lesson today. I'm too pooped." He nodded, wondering if she could read his mind. "Let's have a rain check until tomorrow, okay?" she asked as she rose.

"Sure . . ."

"See you during the afternoon maybe, okay?"

"Yes . . ."

She paused, waiting for him to get up, to walk her to the door, but Willy sat on the floor helpless, a smirk on his face.

"See you . . ." she said uncertainly, starting toward the door without him.

"Yeah . . ."

Alone, he lay back down on the floor, the sun shining into the room she'd left. He was upset, felt so sick to his stomach that he had to swallow several times before the nausea subsided. He remained motionless through the day until darkness came, and Willy, like a sleepwalker, went to his room. Just as he locked the door, he heard his mother's key, but when she called his name, he pretended to be asleep.

By the rush hour that evening, Brooklyn-bound straphangers had known they were in for it. The sun had cooked through all and everything; by afternoon folks were fainting in the stuffy subway trains.

Ole Bertha came into the living room sipping a glass of iced tea and dropped heavily into an armchair.

"Sure is a hot one, all right. I don't know if I can take these summers any more." She sighed.

Willy smiled slightly. "I don't know what you can do about summer. It's going to be here whether you like it or not."

"Hmm, but they're getting worse, I can tell you." She took a long swallow of her drink. "I'll be glad when I get my vacation." He noticed her fidgeting, then feeling under herself.

"What's this?"

His heart skipped as Willy watched his mother scrutinize the object. He recognized the comb immediately. Kathleen used to push it into her hair when she unbraided it and wore it loose. The comb was crescent-shaped with a highly polished surface, genuine tortoise shell, she'd told him.

"It's pretty," Bertha commented, putting down her glass. Willy watched nervously as she ran her fingers along the amber-colored comb.

Oh boy, I hope she doesn't think I bought it for her or something. "It's not mine—"

"I gathered as much."

"It belongs to a friend," he mumbled.

"Uh-huh. A friend?"

What is this, a third degree? "A friend—just a friend," he replied in a loud voice, beginning to get mad at Kathleen for leaving the comb.

His mother was smiling openly now, amused. "Tell me, is your friend—a girl?"

"What do you want to know for?"

Her mouth opened in surprise, then she frowned. "Because I think I should know who's coming into my house when I'm not here. What are you hiding, anyway?"

His eyelids batted rapidly. "I'm not hiding anything." He jerked his shoulders and turned toward his room.

"Oh, no you don't, young man. You're staying right here. I want to know what's going on. You're just a boy—"

"A friend, I can't have a friend?" he shot back.

"You can have as many friends as you want, but I don't see any. How old is this girl?" Her frown deepened.

"Oh, this is crazy—"

"No, it isn't. All kinds of things happen. If you only knew the things—I'm just trying to look out for you—"

"Why? You haven't been looking out all this time," he snapped back without thinking.

He didn't even see it coming, just some streaks of red blinking on and off and the sting on his cheek. She'd actually hit him. He couldn't believe it. She *never* hit him.

"Who do you think you're talking to? You think it's been fun, trying to raise you all this time, glued to the TV like your life depended on it? Just air, just air going to your head, I can tell you that. It hasn't been no sweet party."

For a second he had the old despairing urge to laugh. She did look kind of funny, all huffed and puffed up like that. *Blow the house down* . . . He tried hard to keep back the about-to-burst bubble, catching, holding its center, pain pushing against his throat.

His mother was still talking. "I've tried to make you understand there is a whole world out there that you're going to have to deal with sooner or later, Willy. You think you would try—but no, you just like moping around. I always have to take off work to check things out at your school. And you're going to stand there and tell me I don't look out for you—that I don't care? Maybe you think your father could do better, huh? Just look at what he did to you . . ."

The words had been said; no way to take them back. He watched her eyes close. All the time, all this time she'd never said anything about his father, like she didn't know nothing. How come? A comb? A little ole comb? Or because he didn't want to blab his business? She stood there unmoving. He in turn remained still as a rock, afraid of what was going to happen. But he didn't know what to do about his hands, which kept twisting at the wrists.

"Who's your friend, Willy?" she asked in a soft tone.

"My tutor," he replied dully. His eyes lifted. "Like a teacher. She likes to teach stuff." He tore his eyes away again.

"Your tutor?" his mother echoed in wonder. "Why would you want to hide something like that?" she asked him.

"I don't know . . ." But as he spoke, he knew the answer. He just wanted to do it on his own, that's all . . . to make a friend on his own, to keep it to himself, to guard it. His secret was his protection. You can hold a secret to yourself. Nothing and nobody could touch it. That's how he felt about Kathleen. No one could touch her but him. Now there was no more secret. Now he had no place to keep their friendship.

"Is she helping you?" she asked finally.

"Yes . . ."

"And you like her?"

"Yes."

"Perhaps I'll be able to meet her some day." She smiled hopefully.

Willy moved his eyes away from her. They rested on the speckled comb she had put on the top of the bookcase. He got up, walked slowly, his feet pointing straight, and picked up the comb, placing it safely in his pocket. "I'll give it back to her."

She looked at him a moment longer, then turned toward the kitchen. "It's too hot to cook. I picked us up some Chinese food. Go on and help yourself, Willy. I'm heading for the shower."

Chow mein. Bet it's chow mein again, same ole thing. She knows I like the ribs, but no—pork's not *good* for you, he mimicked her soundlessly. But when he opened one of the neatly bagged boxes, he broke into a grin. Ole Bertha had gone out and bought some good old sweet and sour ribs! Check *that* out!

5

Willy turned over on his stomach, leaning on his elbow to look at the multiplication chart on the back of his notebook. It still made no sense to him. Just a bunch of numbers. He leafed through the book, finding the composition he'd attempted. Kathleen told him he only had to write a paragraph. Only? Whew! At first, Kathleen wanted him to tell about the very best day he had. And he wanted to tell her that he never had one, but he didn't. Finally, he thought of the day he'd gone to the baseball game. Ole Bertha didn't like the idea of him going all the way out to Queens by himself. But who was there to go with?

It had been a long trip. Boring. And, of course, he had to go and get lost. Mixed up, he went too far and had to take another train back, blowing a whole half hour! He had forced himself to have a good time or it would have just been a waste of money.

Willy examined Kathleen's red-penciled corrections on his story, trying to understand why he got so many things wrong. No matter what he did, how hard he worked, it still ended up wrong—not the same wrong as before, a *different* wrong.

He looked up and saw the clock. It was after two—Kathleen was a whole hour late! And she was never late. What could have happened? Maybe she was sick. Maybe he should go over and see if he could help. No, maybe not . . . What can you do for sick people anyway? Like when his mother got a cold or something. All he could do was keep on asking her if she wanted things from the store.

He was really beginning to feel jumpy, his skin itching all over. *Why didn't she come?* He darted to the window, looked through the blinds. He knew he couldn't see her coming from down here, anyway. Maybe he should go upstairs. Only recently he had discovered that the door to the upstairs apartment was unlocked. From the upstairs living room he could see right into the Bowers' kitchen.

As soon as he snuck up, he heard a car, and he rushed to the window. An ambulance stopped in front of the Bowers' house. Wow, there hadn't been a siren, no warning, no nothing. But there it was, like out of nowhere.

At first there was no action in the big white car. He saw that the back door was open, but no one came out and no one went in. Willy's eyes began to ache with strain, his forehead pressed against the grimy windowpane. Then he saw a young man climb out. His face was bark-colored, eyes squinchy like an Oriental. The driver stepped from behind, his big yellowish mustache brushing against his reddish burned skin. The two men struggled together, bringing Mrs. Bowers out in a wheelchair. He was shocked to see how skinny she was. Her eyes—those terrible eyes—were wide open, glaring straight forward at nothing. Her hands were loosely folded in her lap. She didn't move a muscle to steady herself, not even when the chair lurched suddenly to one side.

After they'd gone, Willy felt let down. He couldn't go over to see Kathleen now—that's for sure. For some reason he could not understand, he thought of his grandmother. He'd been a very little boy when she was still alive. She'd looked a lot like his mother, only older, with soft white hair like the halo you saw in church on religious pictures. Before she'd become sick, she was plump and used to hold out her arms, pulling him toward her warm, soft bosom for hugs and kisses. He used to like that. But that's because he was little. And there was a green glass jar she kept on a table near her bed, always full of hard peppermint balls that got smaller and smaller as he sucked.

But then there was that last visit, his grandmother's skin all wrinkled up like spinach leaves. And that smell, so bad that he couldn't stand being near her. Her breasts were flat against her bony ribs, and he wriggled away, wanting to go home, crying. His mother yelled, but he yelled louder. He'd become scared of that old woman who looked a little like his grandmother. Besides, someone had taken away the candy jar . . .

Maybe Mrs. Bowers was going to die, too. How long should he wait? Should he go now? All he wanted to do was see Kathleen. Then he saw the men come back out. He pushed forward to watch the ambulance leave the curb. Then to his astonishment, he saw Kathleen coming toward his house, wearing a big cotton housedress that made her look small inside. Her arms were crisscrossed, hands grasping her elbows. He raced down to meet her.

Kathleen did not look good. Her face had lost some of its rich reddish brown color. "No, I can't come in," she told him in the open doorway before he asked. "My aunt is home . . ."

"I know."

"I'm really sorry—"

"Gosh, Kathleen, it's not your fault. Is she all right?"

"She's doing fine, thank God. The operation was successful." To Willy, it seemed the sparkle was gone from her eyes. "I have to go back, now," she whispered, as if someone were around to hear, "get her settled. I'll see you tomorrow." She turned, heading back quickly before he could reply.

Tomorrow came and Kathleen did not, nor did she come on the following day. Willy continued to wait. Yeah—waiting, *again*. He felt the old resentment climbing up inside his chest, the way it had been with Hunt. The waiting. The no-show. Suppose—suppose she never came again? His pulse was beating wild. Maybe she even went back home, and she'd never said good-bye!

Wait a minute, suppose that crazy woman is holding Kathleen there inside that old spooky house? A prisoner! He'd have to go rescue her. Oh, why doesn't she come!

The days, the nights came and went as Willy kept painful count. He'd totaled five days and nights. Then late in the afternoon, as a hazy drizzle settled into a breathless day, he went outside to the backyard and balanced on a broken concrete slab. A layer of moisture clung to his face and his body, reaching into the folds of his clothing. He looked over at her yard, as he'd done countless times during that week. This time he saw her coming.

Kathleen was wearing one of his very favorite dresses, a sheer green dress that gathered in a bunch below her belt. She had not braided her hair, and it hung loose and tangled as if she hadn't had time to comb it. She surprised him when she almost walked past him with just a nod.

"Say, Willy, let's go for a walk, okay?" He followed silently behind her, along the walk leading to the front. He felt scared. Something bad was going to happen—that's for sure. He *knew* it.

By the time they'd gotten to the candy store, the drizzle had just about evaporated. One step inside, and he realized the timing was wrong. A whole bunch of kids were inside the store, their voices loud and shrill. Fists were held high, squeezing dollar bills and coins; kids jumping around, wanting to be waited on. Willy wanted to suggest they go elsewhere, but Kathleen had slipped onto one of the new stools that had replaced the seatless shafts. Her face was lost in thought. It's taking too long—taking too long for her to say something . . .

"Willy . . ." she began in the same whispering voice she had used before. "I don't know how else to tell you, but to come right out and say it." She gave a little sigh.

His eyes were caught by a spunky little girl arguing with the store owner.

"I gave you the money! I did! I did! Three quarters,

four dimes and a nickel." The man kept trying to snatch the dripping ice-cream cone from her, but the girl managed to keep it just out of his reach. All the other kids were laughing, having a great time until the man came from behind the counter, cursing. "I'll tell your parents, you rotten little bums!" But they'd already beaten him to the door.

"I am going home tomorrow."

He heard her, heard her voice, heard the words, but he knew he hadn't heard her right, so he waited patiently for her to repeat, to correct.

"What kind of sodas you all want this time?" the man asked, still rolling his eyes at the door.

"Two Cokes."

"No Cokes. Mountain Dew, that's all . . ." Willy figured it would be nasty-tasting and wanted to ask Kathleen to go somewhere else, the park, maybe. But the man had already shuffled to the refrigerated case and was removing two cans.

"I know how disappointed you must be, Willy. It was so unexpected. I thought surely I would be here, at least for the whole summer."

The tom-tom beat began heavily behind his ribs. She wasn't changing. She was going on with it. "My aunt decided to get a helper from the agency." She shrugged. "Which is probably the best thing, considering. She'll have professional care. I'll have to go back home, to the islands anyway, now . . ." She seemed to be talking too fast. He could hardly keep up.

A tremendous pressure began at the base of his neck,

funneling through his head and settling between his eyes. For a moment she was distorted, twisting wildly like a mirror in an amusement park. He blinked several times before she straightened out again.

"I received a letter from my mother this morning that said my younger brother's in trouble with the authorities. He was running with the wrong kind of boys even before I left. I—I am really needed at home . . ."

His face opened. "B—but, Kathleen—you can't—"

Her head sagged, the tangled hair in ropes across her face. "I knew how you'd feel, Willy—but there is nothing I can do. I am sorry, truly sorry, believe me . . ."

"Kathleen . . . please don't . . ."

"Willy, but you *knew*," she went on wretchedly. "You knew I would have to return home sooner or later." Her voice was small. "It's just that it's sooner . . ."

He stared at her through blurring eyes, through tears that rolled down over his cheekbones. I didn't know—I didn't know a damn thing! He screamed at her in anguished silence. I need you! They don't need you! He felt like dropping down on his knees, to plead with her not to go, but he felt paralyzed. He couldn't move at all. Suddenly he wanted to be in his room, to be inside it, to pull the walls over his head and wrap himself in them, safe, warm . . . safe, warm . . .

He looked down at a little boy, a little boy playing in white heat. Whrr—whrr—his toy plane cut through the air, swooping down, up again, across, back, sailing, sailing. He recognized him, yes, he did. Little Willy Palmer, all alone in bright sun. The cobblestone street turned gold, glistening, wonderfully shining. He wanted to be that kid again, yes, he did. Uh-huh, uh-huh, I won't grow up—I won't grow up—

"Willy, Willy! Are you all right? God—" As her voice reached him, the little boy swooped back into a little bitty hole. Willy looked at Kathleen's face, and, for a terrible moment, he wondered who she was.

Then he knew, knew the truth that smashed against the small of his back. He pushed himself from the stool awkwardly, hardly able to stand, then hopped from one foot to the other, holding himself.

"I gotta go—I have to go—"

"Willy!"

"Don't you understand!" he yelled. "I have to go to the bathroom!" He fled from the store without looking back.

6

At last, Willy was in his room, the room that always waited there patiently, faithfully in soft dimness. Its four walls hugged him, promised to hide him, to cloak him, to keep him from danger. The shaded darkness cooled him and calmed his hurting thoughts. His room let him forget, and that made it a friend. He wished he never had to leave its safety where all his things were—his radio, his stereo, his TV, his records . . . The room kept him from falling— falling into the deep hole that waited for him beyond, outside, in the danger zone.

Sleep came only because he didn't have the strength to resist. He ate, drank, slept without straining. He was obedient. He came when his mother called. He smiled vacantly and accepted the food she prepared for him. Sometimes, when she spoke to him, it seemed to Willy that her voice echoed from the far end of a long tunnel. He couldn't make out the words, but it didn't matter. He'd smile at her, and it was okay.

Kathleen was a different story. Her image would flash on without any warning. Her eyes were alive, dancing. Then her face would sweep away, just as suddenly, leaving him with the emptiness. He longed for the face to stay, to hang there like a scene would do sometimes on TV. Afterward, he'd want to cry. Sometimes he did.

Maybe three days had passed, maybe a month. Willy wasn't quite sure. Then one smoldering evening when the heat was so bad that steam came off the pavement, he knew if he kept laying there, he'd melt a hole right through the mattress. He was glad ole Bertha had taken herself to a movie—for the air-conditioning, he bet. Tried to get him to go—no way! It may be hot, not hot enough to start going to the movies with his mother again like a little kid. He lifted his head in the darkness of the shrouded room. Balanced on one raised elbow, he thought about the freezing milk in the refrigerator, sinking back in disgust as he recalled he'd finished it. Just iced water left.

Maybe there was some orange juice in the freezer. He hated making that stuff; half the thick liquid always slid down the sides of the bottle when he was trying to pour it in, down into the waiting drain.

He tried to ignore the dryness in his throat. Leaning over, he turned on the TV and realized it was the middle of the regular season. He had hardly seen any of the games!

He watched the man at bat swing on the first ball. Strike one! The second was a huge crack, the camera following the wide curve of the ball through the air. A home run! Wow! Last summer this time he was jumping all over the room like a freakin' kangaroo and whistling through his fingers like crazy. Now he'd learned to cool out, like Cal would do. A commercial cut in, and he sucked his teeth disgustedly, getting up to turn down the sound. He leaned back to watch a happy, but now silent, group of players all sweaty and smiling. Without music or words, the grinning and back-slapping was phoney-baloney.

One of the players, teeth startling white against a purplish black face, grabbed a few bottles and passed them around. The camera focused on a guy with an orange towel around his neck. His head was swung back, swallowing, his face alight with pleasure. Then the camera pulled back as the others began to dump beer on one another's heads. Beer! Crazy stuff. Beer supposed to taste so good, according to them, but he knew it tasted bad—that's for sure.

The white announcer was back on the screen, so he leaned forward to raise the volume only to find that the game was over, over with that home run. The score had broken a tie at the bottom of the ninth, and everybody was going wild.

Willy couldn't believe it . . . They were running the same commercial all over again! There they go, grinning, backslapping, ass-hitting, and passing around the bottle. Froth ran down their hands. The laughing and the music seemed to mix all together, the gulping, the sweating, and the colors blending. The pause that refreshes—a man's drink. Hmph!

In the kitchen Willy swung open the refrigerator door. No Minute Maid neither. Then he spotted the six-pack between his mother's peach yogurt and wheat germ. He stared curiously at the small bubbles. He examined the label, *Champ* (like Ali) and *ale, Champ-ale*. Looks just like

strawberry soda, he thought, with a grin. *Pink Champale.*
He slipped one of the bottles from its cardboard holder,
examining it curiously. Maybe it wouldn't taste as bad as
regular beer. Besides, the coldness felt good in his hand.

As he carried the bottle back to his room, Willy rolled
it against his navel; the icy smoothness made his skin feel
all prickly and nice. Uncapping the bottle, he drew the
liquid into his mouth, floating his tongue inside. "Ughh—"
Should have known. Tastes terrible! But excitement was
building. Sneaking stuff was fun—like playing hooky, same
difference. He took another swallow.

When Willy tipped the bottle to his mouth again, he
was mildly surprised to find it empty. Already? That's
funny . . . He wondered if he should go for another.

On the trip back to the kitchen, he noticed how pretty
and hazy everything looked. He'd almost finished off the
third bottle when it slipped from his hand and crashed
against the kitchen linoleum. Willy looked sadly at the
splintered glass and the widening pink pool circling his
sneakers. Mop—he thought vaguely—maybe I should get
a mop. Instead he dropped down on the floor beside it,
pulled off his T-shirt, and threw it over the spill.

Willy grabbed the last bottle, not bothering to put on
the lights. The full moon coming through the window gave
the room a pale, watery look. He flopped down on his bed
and gazed at the moon edging the clouds in a brilliant
outline. In the heavens he saw the slow parade begin:
curving, slanting, rolling shapes floating majestically across
the sky. He watched the clouds change formation, taking
their own sweet time before beginning to play with the

man in the moon. Willy felt happy, like he'd risen some-how, gone up to meet the parade, and floated dreamily along.

His hand closed absently around the smooth warm bottle, and he twisted the tin cap with one fast turn. The bubbles freed the image of Kathleen from inside him. Imp-ishly, she darted up, giggling at him, skipping weightlessly in and out, tumbling through wads of shifting clouds.

He heard the beat of a drum—drums of Africa. He stood on the mountaintop with Kwami, his brother of blood, listening for messages. Kwami. Kwami's arm was about his shoulders, pointing to the lion. Slay the lion, my brother. And Willy wasn't scared. He was a warrior! The muffled drums became louder, too loud. Kwami began to fade away as the beats increased. And he was falling, falling fast into inky blackness, his head spinning, his lungs gasp-ing for air. A hot mush was running from his nostrils as the drums pounded against his temples—banging louder. He tried hard, so hard, to resist, but he could not keep himself from waking up.

He bolted upright, then slumped back as pain crushed his temples. The room was pitch black, and he felt damp-ness beneath his buttocks—Jesus, he'd peed on himself!

"Willy! Willy! For the last time, get this door open!"

Again, he tried to sit up, but collapsed weakly. He felt sick, really sick—and a sweetish-sour smell told him he'd thrown up. He shook his head vigorously and suc-ceeded in swinging his legs over the side of the bed. He stood up, swaying unsteadily. He'd hardly opened the door when a hand shot through the space. The ceiling light came on, damn near blinding him.

His mother looked terrible. What's wrong with her? Her face was all puffy and swollen, as if she'd been crying. He'd never in his life seen her cry.

He was astonished by the mess around him. Empty bottles were on the floor, the dresser. His table lamp was lying dismally on its side. And he couldn't understand why his records were all out of their jackets. His thoughts were swirling, tumbling, trying to put the torn pieces together.

But he was too sick. Sick as a dog . . .

"What happened here?" his mother demanded, her eyes sweeping around the room. When he didn't answer, she said in a low voice, "This place stinks. Open the window and get some air in here."

"What happened?" He asked *her*, this time.

"Nothing much. Looks like you got drunk. Drank up more than eight bottles. Some empties are in the kitchen," she said tonelessly. "Clean up this place, and I'll talk to you later. God. I can't even go to see a movie without all hell breaking loose."

He stood there aching and shamed, staring at the door she slammed behind her.

It took Willy a long time to clean up the mess, his mind still shrouded in confusion. He peeled off the wet bedcovers, carried out all the bottles, and tried to get the vomit off his pillow with disinfectant. Finally, he took a shower and put on clean clothes. He went to the kitchen, knowing he couldn't possibly eat, but knowing he should wait there.

And eventually he heard her shoes hard against the wooden floor of the hall.

Ole Bertha was fully dressed, her head tied with a piece of African cloth he remembered she'd bought a couple of years ago. "Just what were you trying to prove?" she asked gravely.

"Nothing, I—"

"Then why did you do it?"

"Do what?"

"Oh, Willy, don't play games with me," she retorted angrily. "Why did you drink up all that beer?"

He thought a while.

"Maybe I wanted to feel better . . ." he said, uncertainly.

"Well, do you?"

"No, not really—not now, anyway."

She nodded, her eyes on his face. "Well, I hope you've learned your lesson." He wasn't sure what lesson he was supposed to have learned. Maybe it was that if you get drunk, you can feel good, but you end up feeling real bad.

"Get yourself some breakfast—no, coffee. Put on some water to make yourself some coffee."

He did a double take. She knew darn well he didn't drink coffee. Made him nervous.

She started out of the room, then stopped short. "Oh, I forgot to tell you," she said dully. "Your friend was by here last night—what's her name?"

A loud roar rushed past his ears. He felt sick again, dizzy. "What? What?"

"Your friend, Kathy, I think. She was here last night."

"She was here?" he asked hoarsely. He was going to pass out, right then and there.

"Yes. Said she came to tell you good-bye, but I couldn't rouse you. I couldn't get in your room. That lock is coming off *today*."

"But—but I thought she'd gone . . ."

"Now, Willy, that's just silly. Why would she go without seeing you?"

He leaned against the stove after she'd left the room. He'd missed Kathleen, missed seeing her. She'd come to see him, and he was out like a light. God! He had to get out—had to go. Minutes later he was running through the streets of waking Brooklyn.

He turned into a block where there were no houses, just remnants, crumbs of what was once a busy thoroughfare. Broken walls with peeling pastel paint exposing what used to be living rooms, kitchens, and hallways, where families had lived. Loose bricks and broken bottles littered the area, mixed with shattered bits of broken glass, glittering like hundreds of tiny jewels.

In the middle of an empty lot, Willy dropped down on top of the rubble and gazed at the stubborn tufts of grass pushing through the refuse. Then he saw the butterfly—about the biggest butterfly he'd ever seen in his life. It was a lovely shade of orange with black and green patterning on its wings. He watched it balance gracefully on a swaying branch, then fly off to stop, suspended on the breeze. The butterfly was motionless, and so was Willy. He could feel himself straining against moving, and he understood that they were testing each other. Who could last the longest? Just when Willy began to believe the butterfly had been painted on the sky somehow, it fluttered off, zigzagging, sailing away, vanishing from sight altogether.

His spirits dropped again as he heard a rumble. He looked up to see a jet cut through the clouds like a silver bullet. Was she there? Was she on the plane? His head lowered, Willy left the lot and headed for the park.

Without the wind, the lake was serene, smooth as glass. Aluminum boats were piled on the shore upside down, shining in the sun as if they had been carefully scrubbed and put away. The boathouse was closed. He stared out over the water. He was feeling awful. He could picture Kathleen getting into the boat, spreading her skirt wide, then reaching eagerly for the oars. Could row like a natural champ . . .

His eyes fell on a girl approaching, and he looked away. He frowned. As he looked back again, his heart gave a wild leap. The girl looked enough like Kathleen to be her twin! But she was wearing jeans . . . tight jeans. Kathleen never wore pants. The girl was looking at him and smiling. Willy was confused. What's going on?

Now she stood directly in front of him. He couldn't breathe . . .

"Willy?"

He rose slowly to his feet, his mind warning him not to trust what was happening. Your mind could fool you—that's for sure. He knew Kathleen was on that plane he'd seen jetting through the skies. But here she was.

"Kathleen?"

"Yes, it's me, Willy," she said quietly.

It couldn't be. This girl's hair wasn't in braids or loose, but swept up high on her head, and she was wearing lipstick!

She gave a nervous little laugh. "Don't I look nice? My cousin wanted to fix me up, so I let her. Said I needed a New York look to go home with," she said, smiling.

Willy was flabbergasted. It was Kathleen, but she didn't seem like Kathleen at all. And if she was, what was she doing here?

"I was so worried the other day when you ran off," she started. "I didn't know what to do because my aunt and uncle were waiting for me. Uncle decided I should see my cousins before I left the States. So I stayed for a couple of days. When I came back to see you, your mother said you weren't feeling well. Are you feeling better now?"

"Better? Yes, better."

His mind was racing. Maybe she wasn't leaving after all! Maybe she was staying until the end of the summer, maybe even longer . . . Maybe she wouldn't be going home at all!

"Anyway, Uncle found a cheaper fare for tonight, so I was happy knowing I'd be able to see you after all. When I passed by just now, your mother told me you'd taken off somewhere. But I remembered. I remembered the park. And see, I found you." The big grin seemed pasted on her face.

His thoughts scattered like mice. Why should she care about the fare if she was staying? His hand flew up to his mouth. "No, you're not . . ."

The unfamiliar scarlet on her mouth looked like a

blood stain. "Willy, you must understand. I wanted to say good-bye to you. But now less time is available. I have to go back to my cousin's house. They decided to give me a party. Isn't that nice? And I want you to come."

Willy had never known such great tiredness. "I—I don't want to be around people," he said softly.

"It's just family, Willy. Don't be like that," she admonished him.

"You looked for me to say good-bye. Maybe that's what you should do, just say good-bye," he said cruelly.

But he was trying to etch her into his brain—her shining eyes, the length of her neck and wide smile. In his mind, he was undoing the curls that topped her head and dressing her in his favorite outfit, the skirt swelling at her ankles.

She looked so sad that for a second he wanted to change his mind, but it was too late.

"Now, Willy, you must promise to write. And don't you feel shy about your spelling or anything. You know I'll be able to read it."

He nodded his head and rose to his feet clumsily. "It was a good summer . . ." he began.

"Oh, Willy, for me, too," she said warmly.

His hand went out shakily. Kathleen looked down at it. She threw her arms out, pulling him to her, and kissed him lightly on the mouth.

"Good-bye, Willy, you take care."

Don't go—don't go—please don't go, he cried out silently. He watched her walk away, hating the jeans that pushed out her small buttocks, two round curves, like two small basketballs. He tore his eyes away as she reached the exit.

The wood slats of the bench pressed into his back as his eyes brimmed with tears. They always say a man ain't supposed to cry. Some day—just some day he'd find out just who "they" are.

Their wings spread wide, sea gulls glided down on the early morning breeze. Willy listened to the strange craw-craw sounds the birds made as they swooped down into the waves, pulling out small fish with their beaks. He was at peace. He was pleased with himself, glad he'd come down on the beach before anyone else. He felt all alone in the world, except for the birds, the fish, and the sound of the waves.

His mother had come home from work one day and announced she was taking her vacation, asking if he wanted to come along with her to Sag Harbor. Of course, he didn't know what and where that was, but he'd said he'd go, anything to get away from Brooklyn—from re-membering. He smiled to himself, thinking about how the summer heat must have his room like an oven. He was sure glad he decided to come, even though boys his age didn't go traveling around with their mothers.

He hadn't dreamed his mother's boss had a setup like this, a house on a beach. Get to that! And just how many people are invited to spend their vacation with their boss!

Willy hadn't quite made up his mind about Miss

Gaines. He didn't particularly take to her, but he didn't dislike her either. More like he felt it was best to stand away from her a bit if you could. She was a tall, middle-aged woman with straight hair pulled into stiff curls on the back of her neck. Almost always Miss Gaines wore a pantsuit, not that Willy could picture her in a dress or skirt. He suspected he had not been invited. Willy had seen her look of surprise, and the quick frown when she saw him. But he was here, and that was all there was to it.

Another thing about Miss Gaines was that no matter how hot it got, she never seemed to work up even a little bit of sweat. She was cool as a cucumber. Two cools, and too cool. He laughed at his little word game. What she was don't matter no way 'cause she sure enough got a ba-aa-d house.

Sometimes Willy swam in the bay; other times he just sat on the rocks looking out at the boats. People waved as they passed, and he waved back. He liked that. It seemed real friendly. He was having fun, although he wished there was someone with him. His mother preferred to stay in the big house or sit on the porch—patio, she called it—sipping cold drinks and talking. So Willy was on his own. He noticed other kids on the beach, but they seemed to know one another and hang out together. He didn't know how to break through.

There were still times when he thought of Kathleen. No longer would her face pop into his head without warning as it had before. He could now form a clear picture of her and make it stay for a while, her impish expression and laughing eyes. But he could never reproduce her voice—no matter how he tried, she would not speak.

Bet if she'd stayed in the country, she'd be right here with him on the rock, probably acting all school-teacherish, telling him about the life of sea gulls.

The night before, he'd finally got up enough nerve to ask ole Bertha to help him write a letter to Kathleen. Miss Gaines had gone off to see someone down on the other side of the beach. He'd found his mother in the elegant dining room sipping coffee from a dolly cup.

"What's that?" he'd asked, pointing at it and laughing.

"Just to show how much you know," she replied playfully. "This, my dear boy, is a demitasse."

"A demi *who*?"

"It's too bad that some people don't have any culture," she joked, sticking her nose in the air. "This, my fine young man, is the way 'refined' people drink coffee after dinner."

"Really? In that little bitty cup? Can't get much coffee in there—that's for sure. You're going to have to drink at least eight of those things to match up one of the mugs at home."

"Oh, get out of here," she waved him away good-naturedly. But Willy didn't leave.

For most of the day he'd been trying to write the letter himself, checking the spelling in a big dictionary he'd discovered in the back of the house in a room that looked like the library in his neighborhood. But each time he tried to start the letter, it was the same: a sheet of paper made ugly by his terrible uneven scrawl. He'd tried to write in script, but it looked so bad he started printing, and even that looked lousy. He didn't even know if the words made any sense. He should have continued to practice, but it was too hard without Kathleen.

He decided to take the plunge. "Can you write a letter to Kathleen for me?" he asked quickly. "I'll tell you what to say."

His mother appeared not to have heard him, although he knew there was no way she couldn't have. He repeated the question. When her eyes turned toward him, he was startled to see them soft-looking, almost sadlike.

"You want me to write your letter, Willy?"

He hung his head. "Yeah."

"Why don't you do it yourself?"

"You know I can't," he answered wretchedly.

"How do you know that? Have you tried?"

"Yes," he said loudly.

"I know how you feel, Willy, but I won't write your letter. You have to write it yourself."

"I'll tell you what to say, honest—" he pleaded, close to tears.

"She was your teacher, Willy, your friend. She'd appreciate it if you made the attempt . . ."

But he could tell from her voice that she was beginning to soften. All he had to do was keep up the pressure, and she'd break down. "Please—" he began with his best cry-cry voice. "I've tried a lot of times. It just looks so bad—all sloppy, messed up." He dropped his head, watching her from the corner of his eye. She rose slowly, the coffee cup in her hand, and thoughtfully placed it on the saucer.

"Well"—she turned back to him—"let me see the letters, Willy."

Damn. Forget it. "I tore them up," he told her uncertainly.

"You did what!"

"I told you, it was crap!"

"Now, you just watch your mouth, young man!" she exclaimed.

"Okay, okay, but are you going to help me or not?" he asked, impatient.

"I didn't say I wouldn't help you." She thought for a minute. "But I'll tell you how we're going to work this out. You dictate what you want to say. I'll write it down, but you have to copy it in your own handwriting."

Willy thought it over. Yeah, better than nothing. "That's a bet!" he answered happily, jumping up.

"Wait! That's not all. The other condition is that you practice when we get home, just like you would with Kathleen."

"Okay, that's a deal." He'd handle that when he got home.

As it turned out, he didn't have that much to say, really, except how much he missed her . . .

Later on that night, Willy went out to catch fireflies, a nightly routine for him. As much as he liked the early morning, he liked the nighttime even better. He could see all kinds of fantastic shapes—hear the weirdest sounds.

He enjoyed the sound of the crickets best of all, happily listening to their endless monotone.

The fireflies were something else. They'd been blinking at him from the first night, and he was determined to catch some. By the sixth night, he'd become an expert at stalking the bright bugs. He would pretend that a mayonnaise jar filled with them was a lantern lighting his way into the forest of the night. Living lights, how about that . . .

Now he watched an illuminated insect alight on a bush, still as can be. It gave Willy time to plan and calculate, to wait for the right moment. Seconds passed. Then he made his move. Sudden, fast. Got him! He began to track them, like Kwami would have done in the jungle of the darkness. He was Kwami himself. The full moon spilled out silver light for his fairy-tale wonder.

Soon he had more than a dozen twinkling lights transforming the jar into a natural light.

Then he noticed a slight stirring in the shadows. Ice slid down the back of his neck. The bush rustled again. What was it? Fear grabbed at his stomach. An animal? A snake? The lion-drum—

"Who's there!" he demanded, trembling.

"It's just me . . ." said a light, squeaky voice. A boy stood up timidly. His complexion was so dark that Willy could see only his glasses at first. What a sight! His swimming trunks were so large that Willy wondered how he could swim without losing them.

"I'm sorry—" the boy apologized. "I just wanted to see how you caught them . . ."

"Shouldn't sneak up on somebody like that," Willy said harshly. "You could get yourself done in. I'd hate to tell what happens if you pulled a stunt like that in Bed-Stuy."

"Where's Bed-Stuy?" the boy asked, curious.

"You never heard of Bed-Stuy?" Willy asked, incredulous. "It's in Brooklyn—and it's a monster."

"A monster?" His eyes were like saucers behind the rims of his glasses.

"Not a real monster." Willy sucked his teeth. "It's just the kind of place you can get real hurt if you don't keep your eyes open."

The boy's neck pushed out from his shoulders. "Well, I wanted to see how you caught the fireflies." He stepped closer. Willy saw that the boy was young, maybe about eight or nine years old. He wondered what he was supposed to do now.

"Okay, I'll show you. Follow me," Willy said, feeling older, smarter. "You really got to move in fast on them. They know you're out there—that's for sure. And they get away if you don't jump in right on them. Do you have a bottle?"

The boy shook his head no. "That's okay. We'll just have to share this one. Now, check this out—" The expression came from the story of Cal. "You gotta snatch at them when you see one; close your fist real tight. I'll have to show you how to get them in the bottle so they won't get away. Then you have to get the cover on without losing none. I already punched holes in it so they can breathe."

The boy nodded eagerly, eyeing a firefly hovering above Willy's head. "There's one!" he shouted, leaping for it and almost knocking Willy off balance. He missed it.

"Don't worry. You'll get the hang of it," Willy said, enjoying his new sense of importance.

They had a good time together, playing catch with the bugs that lit up and blinked off. Willy learned the boy's name was Jimmy. After a while they moved down toward the edge of the bay, dropping down into sand grayed by the dark night.

"They have a big boat down the other end," Jimmy said in the dimness. "Sometimes they take me with them."

"Oh, yeah?" Willy responded, wondering who he was talking about.

"On the weekends. It's the only time they use the boat, so you'll have to wait."

Willy raised up on his elbow. "Who you talking about?"

"My parents," Jimmy replied, looking at him. "I stay out here mostly by myself. A woman takes care of me and cleans the house . . ." He looked out toward the invisible horizon.

Willy's eyes widened. A maid, that's what he means. "Your parents rich?"

The boy took a few minutes to think about it. "I don't think so. Just that my father's a lawyer and busy all week. And my mother works, too. The woman takes care of me until they come on the weekends." He brightened. "But we always had the house here and the boat."

"You go fishing in it, too?"

"Naw, you're talking about a different kind of boat.

Those boats have seats in the back and a place where you put fishing rods."

Willy was sorry he'd asked since now it was Jimmy showing that he knew stuff. He changed the subject. "It must be really fun to live out here all summer long, right?"

"It's okay, but there's nobody to play with. The kids out here are cousins or they're in the same class—or their parents know each other." The boy picked up a twig and began to draw on the sand. Uh-huh, so he had problems, too.

"When do you want to go out in the boat," Jimmy was asking him. "Saturday or Sunday?"

Willy shrugged. "Don't matter . . ." he answered, trying to picture the kind of boat it would be.

Jimmy looked blindly into the darkness, a strange smile on his face. Funny little dude, Willy thought, borrowing another word from Cal. "But tomorrow is Thursday. Maybe we can go swimming."

"I can't swim," the boy announced. Willy looked at him in disbelief. Living way out here and can't swim? A sense of elation swept over him. Here was his chance.

"I'll teach you," he offered brightly. "We'll meet right here in the morning, but you've got to be early. Nobody's out then, so you won't have to worry about nobody looking," he explained.

"Okay."

Then Jimmy's expression changed. He sat up abruptly. "What time is it?"

Willy shrugged his shoulders. "Oh, maybe around ten or eleven."

"Hey!" The boy scrambled to his feet, sending sand

flying up into Willy's face. His eyes were huge behind the lenses of his glasses.

"I'm sorry, but it's time. I've got to go—"

Willy was dumbfounded. "What's going on? Wait—"

"No," the boy said, starting off. "It's late." His eyes were shining in panic.

"Who? What?"

"No, you don't know what happens—" His body twisted for flight, and he was gone, disappearing into the night.

Willy was on the beach by a quarter to seven the next morning, scolding himself because he hadn't given his new friend an exact time. But he was prepared to wait. He squatted down near the shore.

He watched the tide. After a while he began making letters in the wet sand. "Stupid," he said aloud. Should have watched where he'd rushed off to. Think the kid could have known about him—that he had problems, no friends? How could he? No way . . . but where *was* he?

During the morning, Willy often looked back at the row of houses, his eyes examining each one, straining to see Jimmy. Other people came out to swim, sail, or to board their yachts. Three hours passed before Willy gave in to his anger. And that was only because of the waiting—waiting, again. He *hated* it. He hated the slow crawling minutes, never being sure if people would show up. First Hunt, waiting for him—then Kathleen, waiting for her—now Jimmy, this little kid, waiting for him, too.

Around noon Willy gave up. He wasn't coming.

"I don't care—you think I care, but I don't!" he

shouted at the houses. He ran along the shore, water and sand stinging his ankles.

Near the end of the beach, he turned sharply and cut deep into the water, his arms digging furiously in and out, out and in, farther, farther, heading toward the line that divided ocean from sky.

Now he got over his disappointments easier. Before, he'd
be low down and miserable for days. But he'd slept well
that night, maybe because he was so bushed. He'd swum
far out, beyond the sand bar, returning out of breath, his
limbs aching.

Two days passed. He rose at five in the morning and
was ready for his swim by six. It was getting boring, like
everything else, but there was nothing else to do. The water
was warm, soothing his skin as he waded in slowly. It was
so clear he could see right down to the bottom. He pushed
farther out, looking down through the water at the sea-
shells and the patterns of colored stones. Then he plunged
in, trying to keep his eyes open to examine the underwater
scene more closely. But his eyelids burned, and he closed
them tight. Lifting easily, he turned on his back, rocking
on the salty waves. He was glad that guy at camp had
worked with him all one summer until he learned the
strokes. Dick—that was his name. He hadn't thought of
him for a long time. Dick wasn't an adult, just a teenager.
If it hadn't been for the swimming, it would have been
just another summer.

After his swim, Willy took a nap on the sand. It was near lunchtime when he awoke and wandered along the shore. He spotted a small crab scrambling across the grainy sand and bent to watch its journey.

"Hi, Willy."

Willy spun around. Jimmy! His friend's expression shocked him. It was the saddest face he'd ever seen. What was the matter with him?

"I'm sorry I didn't make it back . . ." Jimmy was avoiding Willy's eyes. Willy waited for more, but nothing else came.

"Well, you want to go swimming this morning?" he asked, trying not to think about being stood up.

Jimmy's head jerked around sharply. Willy might have said, "Let's jump off the Brooklyn Bridge," from the scared look that appeared on Jimmy's face.

"No . . ." He dropped his head. "I can't find my bathing suit."

What a dumb excuse! "Ah, c'mon. We'll get you a suit. I have an extra one. About the same size as yours," he commented, grinning as he thought of the first time he'd seen Jimmy all swallowed up in the oversized trunks.

He was happy to see Jimmy, relieved really. Yet, Willy wanted to ask why he hadn't shown up.

It never occurred to Willy that something could have happened to his little friend, not until now. He looked at the boy closely, wondering if something did happen.

"So, what are you going to do?" Willy asked.

The boy considered for a while, then, "I'll use your trunks," he answered, shrugging.

"Great!"

Silently, they walked toward Miss Gaines' summer house. The midday sun gave it a fresh brightness, the windows reflecting the baby-blue color of the sky. Ole Bertha was seated on the patio, with a sliced mango on a small round table in front of her.

She looked up and saw him. "Willy, come taste this fruit. It's delicious." She smiled at Jimmy.

"No thanks. Don't want any." He motioned to his friend. "This is Jimmy."

"Well, Jimmy, how are you?" It was obvious that his mother was pleased to see him with a friend. But his mind was still on Jimmy, worrying about what was bothering him. And now Jimmy was acting even more weird, like he didn't want to meet Willy's mother.

"His parents have a boat," Willy offered.

"Oh?" His mother looked interested. "What kind of boat is it?"

"I don't know. Maybe I'll get to see it today. His parents come on weekends." He looked over to Jimmy. "They're not here yet, are they?"

"No."

"Well, it's Saturday . . ." His forehead wrinkled in new concern as he saw how uneasy Jimmy had become.

"They're not here yet," Jimmy said, his voice low.

"I'll probably get a ride when they get here," Willy commented, his enthusiasm waning.

"It's a sailboat," Jimmy informed them, his eyes still on his feet.

"Well, enjoy yourselves, boys," his mother said, smiling as she went back to her fruit. They got the suit and went back down to the beach.

As they slid under the waves, Willy's hand automatically reached out toward Jimmy's small form, ready to show him how to balance himself on top of the water and use the waves to his advantage.

"Hey!" The scream ripped across the waves.

What the hell? Dammit, now he knew something was wrong—something was bad wrong. "I gotta go back . . ." Jimmy groaned painfully, batting at the waves, his legs struggling, his nose running.

"What's the matter? I keep asking you!" Willy hollered after him.

"Nothing . . . nothing . . . a cramp, I got a cramp," Jimmy shouted over his shoulder.

"How could you have a cramp? You haven't *done* anything!" Jimmy raced out of the water, running toward the houses, then stopped abruptly and dropped face down on the sand. As Willy approached warily, he saw the boy's jerking shoulders and knew Jimmy was crying. Sand granules coated his legs, reminding Willy of his mother coating raw chicken legs for frying.

"God, Jimmy, what's happening to you?" The boy's sobs grew louder. Willy felt helpless, useless. He didn't know what to do. He reached out to touch him, but Jimmy yanked his shoulder back as if Willy had fire in his hand.

Then it dawned on Willy. He should have known. He jumped up. "You hurt!" he said accusingly. "And you hurt all over, too." Willy got close to the boy, noticing for the first time the welts on his thin body.

"Who did it! Who beat you up?" Willy demanded hotly.

"Nobody! Nobody! Are you crazy?" Jimmy cried, rolling away from Willy's touch. "Anyway, why do you care? *Your* mother is here," Jimmy spat out, the tears beginning to dry in grayish streaks on his dark skin.

His mother? He wants his mother? Maybe it's his father who beats him up . . . But he's not even here. It's got to be the big boys. They always pick on kids. Well, they'd get them. He wasn't scared like he used to be.

"Listen, Jimmy. Don't worry. I'll get them. They don't scare me."

Jimmy looked up, perplexed. "Who?"

Willy waved his hand. "Oh, I know, think I don't know? Some kids are giving you a rough time, right?"

Jimmy stared at him, his eyes bigger than ever, as if they took up his whole face. Now it seemed Jimmy was the one studying *him*, trying to figure *him* out. The boy rose to his feet with effort. "I'm going inside. Tired."

"Want me to go with you?" Willy asked, still feeling anxious. The boy shook his head as he moved away toward the house, the only one set inside a surrounding wall. Willy remained where he was. Okay, so at least he now knew where Jimmy lived. Wait—he'd need a reason to go there. The bathing suit, right. After all, he'd only loaned it to him. But he wouldn't go right away. That wouldn't be cool. Instead, he walked back to his own place. There's time. There'll be time . . .

Later that evening he went to the house. Instead of Jimmy, a woman opened the door. She was tall and young-looking, her raised chin making her seem as tall as the door. Her eyelashes were painted thick and her eyebrows penciled in. She didn't wear lipstick.

"What do you want?" Her man's voice startled him.

"I'm looking for Jimmy," he said, regaining his composure.

"He isn't here," came the answer.

"What? But—"

"He's not here," the woman repeated stonily, her eyes narrowed.

"Well, he told me to meet him here about this time." The fib came easily.

Under the paint, her eyes changed.

"Perhaps he is asleep. Come in."

Willy stepped into the front room. Inside, the woman looked down on him again. She was dark-skinned, but he didn't think she was an American, not the way she talked.

Before he knew it, she disappeared into another room.

He took the time to look around him. The white tiles on the floor were spotless, but there was scarcely any real furniture. He bet twenty people could sit on the pepper-red sofa. The two chairs were modern looking, and big pillows were piled on the floor. If Jimmy was rich, his folks didn't put no money in no furniture.

"He's coming," she announced flatly. Her way of speaking prevented a reply, even thank-you. Funny how she made him think of Mrs. Bowers.

"I figured it was you," Jimmy said, coming across the room, his feet taking small little measured steps. He was wearing yellow shorts and a brown T-shirt so close to the color of his skin that he looked bare from the waist up.

"Yeah." Willy grinned. "My bathing suit. My other one's wet."

"Oh. It's on the line in the back."

As they walked out to the backyard, Willy could see Jimmy grimacing with pain.

"You know, Jimmy. You might as well tell me the kids who did it. It's not right."

"I don't want to talk about it," he answered glumly.

"Why not?"

"I just don't—that's all," he said stubbornly.

"Well—"

"What's it to you, anyway!" he exclaimed hotly.

"I should know!" Willy retorted. "They piss on me all the time, too!"

"Nobody's pissing on me!"

Willy didn't want them to have a shouting match. "Well," he said, quieter, "who hurt you?"

Then suddenly Willy looked up and saw her standing across the lawn at the back door. He saw Jimmy's glance, his eyes darkening with fear. All at once, Willy knew. It was her! It was the woman! *She's the one who beats him!*

Be cool. Don't show anything. Be cool . . . "C'mon, Jimmy. Let's go for a walk."

"No. No, I can't . . ." He was terrified. He kept looking at the woman, then looking away, then back again, as if he were watching two people playing catch in a small space.

"Don't be scared. She's not going to hurt you," Willy told him, glaring at the woman.

"She'll get me, she warned me . . ." He began to cry.

Willy felt lousy. "C'mon over to my place."

"No, I tell you . . ." he begged.

"Well, then, I'm going to bring back my mother," Willy informed him, determined.

"No, don't go—it'll be bad."

"Well, then, come on with me. You can't stay here now, anyway." Willy looked at the doorway. It was empty.

"Don't worry about pajamas or stuff like that. I'll fix you up."

A breeze cooled them as they walked briskly down the beach. Willy felt he'd taken care of stuff really good.

Ole Bertha did just what Willy hoped she would do: she got Miss Gaines to let Jimmy stay overnight. He wasn't sure how to explain the real problem to his mother, so he decided to put it off until later. He got the folding cot from the basement. Then he went for a towel and some aspirin, returning to find his friend fast asleep on the cot, eyeglasses askew on his narrow face. Smiling, Willy took them off and placed them on his bureau, then went down to join his mother.

He put on a real serious face, straightened his shoulders, and tried to think of the best way to start the story— well, from the beginning. Or should he tell her about the housekeeper first, then go back to how he figured it out? Maybe it would be better to tell her what happened in the water and go on from there . . .

But Bertha wasn't on the porch or in the living room. He headed for her room. He found her all dressed up.

"Where are you going now?" he asked with sullen disappointment.

"A party, at one of the other houses."

"But why *now*?" A scowl deepened on his face.

Her shoulders slumped. "Oh, Willy, don't start your stuff. I haven't been out since we got here."

"I know, but I wanted to tell you something . . ."

"It'll have to wait—that's all," she told him, bending toward the mirror with her lip gloss.

"I guess it'll have to . . ." he responded glumly and walked away.

The next morning both his mother and his friend slept late. He pulled on his trunks and went for his early-morning swim. People were already out in the water. This Sunday was going to be crowded. If Jimmy's parents were coming this weekend, it would have to be today. But he recalled his friend telling him sometimes they didn't come at all. Actually, they could be at the house already. Should he go look? Well, he could see if there was a car in the driveway at least, although he was really scared of seeing that witch. Just like Mrs. Bowers, but worse . . . Nah, he'd just wait. No need looking for trouble. He'd just go in for his swim, and ole Bertha would be up when he came back.

Later on, as Willy and his mother sat in the peacefulness of the late Sag Harbor morning, he told her the long, rambling story that began with fireflies and ended with how he got Jimmy to beat it out of that house and away from the woman.

Willy's mother listened quietly, her eyes on her son's face. She showed surprise first, then shock. Willy watched her hand move to her heart, then her fingers touching her lips as if to still them. Willy felt strangely triumphant, as if he'd been given some important mission to carry out—the changes in his mother's face making him realize that he had succeeded.

After lunch, Willy stayed with Jimmy while his mother, accompanied by Miss Gaines, went over to Jimmy's house. When they returned, Miss Gaines looked cross, and ole Bertha simply looked sad.

"Your parents want you, Jimmy. They came in early this morning."

Jimmy started to tremble. "No, don't worry. The woman is gone," Willy's mother assured him. "The authorities have been contacted and will take care of her." Her face was full of compassion. "She'll never hurt you again."

Bertha smiled at Willy. "The Boones—that's Jimmy's parents—they wanted to thank you personally. But they're tired and upset. Said to tell you they are going to take the boat out tomorrow and want you to come with them."

"Okay," he said.

Jimmy shot a last look at his friend. "See you later?"

"Bet."

To Willy, Jimmy looked bigger as he walked away. That's one thing he'd never understand, how people could look small one minute and big the next.

# 9

Two weeks had come and gone so quickly. Willy felt it had been more like a few days—but with a whole bunch of stuff going on in between. Everything was packed and ready. Miss Gaines drove them to the station and shook hands stiffly. She was like that, stiff. He hadn't really seen her show any *real* feeling at all, even when the business with Jimmy was going on.

A wave of depression swept over him as he thought of the ugly subway caves, the incessant noise, and the unbearable humidity that he was returning to. Hardened citified faces, unguarded streets, drunks, and the roaches marched into his mind. Already he was yearning for the sea gulls, the boats, and Jimmy.

Jimmy had become another boy after his parents had come. Willy's mother told him later that the courts had taken the woman's children away because she'd beaten them up, too. His mother tried to explain that the woman was really sick and couldn't help it.

Bullshit! The woman was bad—bad! Should put her butt in jail—that's what! It was *Jimmy* who had needed the help.

Going out on the boat that day had been great. It was a twenty-two-foot open boat, Mr. Boone had explained. It had two sails, the big sail in the back, and space enough for four or five people.

Sailing was different than he'd thought. At first nothing much happened. He wondered if they were just going to sit there, but then the wind picked up, and before he knew it they were gliding through the water. It was an unbelievable feeling: a sense of freedom, of not caring about anything else in the world. A sailboat wasn't anything like a motorboat that made a lot of noise and plunged roughly through the waters. It was very, very quiet.

Although stuff could go on, too, like anywhere else. At one point, Jimmy's father changed direction and shouted suddenly, "Willy, duck or you'll get hit by the boom!" He'd ducked fast.

Jimmy's father was a nice-looking man with glasses and gray at his temples. Sometimes he laughed, a heavy belly-king of laugh, while Jimmy's mother only smiled a little. Maybe she'd been thinking about everything Jimmy had gone through—and nobody had suspected, not even a little bit. Maybe she even felt guilty about what had happened.

But as hard as he tried to fight against it, the sights, sounds, smells, and memories began to fade as the train came closer and closer to the city. The polluted air of New York gave him a headache.

Ole Bertha took off for the supermarket, so Willy went to his room, throwing open the windows to get rid of the mustiness. But even his room didn't make him feel any better about being back home. For a few seconds he thought about going to the park. Maybe, he didn't know . . . no. She was gone. As he slammed the iron gate behind him, he stepped into some dog mess. "Damn," he said in disgust. "Now I know I'm home."

Later, he spotted Mr. Bowers and wanted to duck him, not so much because he didn't want to see his old friend, but because it would force him to deal with really being back home: the final end of Sag Harbor and Jimmy. But it was too late; Mr. Bowers was coming toward him.

"Hello there, Willy. Good to see you, my boy. How was the trip?" he said, closing his gate behind him.

"It was okay, really great," Willy replied, smiling. "How've you been, Mr. Bowers?"

"Well, not too bad for an old man. Glad I saw you, too." He was searching in his pockets, in the side pockets of his overalls, then his shirt pocket. "I have something for you." He looked up, shaking his head at nothing, then found what he was looking for in his back pocket. He held up the lavender envelope. Willy's heart flipped-flopped. Kathleen!

"I knew you'd want this straight away," Mr. Bowers said with a toothy grin, handing it to him.

Willy's hands twitched slightly as he took the envelope. Willy peered at the old man. He didn't look all that good. A dark reddish color coated his face, and his eyes were more smoky than ever. Suddenly he realized Mr. Bowers was waiting for him to open the envelope, to read the letter, even though it was private. Why should he want to know something personal? But Willy couldn't wait to see what Kathleen had written. He tore the envelope open, pulling out the faded sheet. Immediately, his excitement sank to disappointment. There was only one short page.

He thrust the letter toward Mr. Bowers. The old man looked at the sheet, then at Willy, confused.

"You want to read it?" Willy asked him.

"Nonsense! It's your letter."

Willy sighed, smiling weakly. "It's all right, honestly. I want you to."

Mr. Bowers hesitated, then mumbled, "All right . . ." He lifted the letter from Willy's fingers, his own hands shaking, tired or something.

*My dear Willy,*

*I hope this letter finds you well and in good spirits. Our trip was safe, but a bit scary because of the turbulence . . .* (What was that?)

*But I am thankful that the Creator guided us safely. I was very happy to see my mother and my sisters and brothers. I do have a great deal of work to catch up on and hardly enough time to do it. Please give my regards to your mother.* (Mr. Bowers paused, coughing.)

*I hope you are keeping up with your work. I have faith in you. I await hearing from you.* (Oh, she didn't get his letter, yet.)

*I remain your loving friend, Kathleen.*

It was a nice enough letter, sounding like Kathleen, but too short, not saying any of the things he wanted to hear, like things happening in the West Indies, just worried about his work. Might as well have asked him straight out, "Are you reading?" just like his father did that one time. He glanced at Mr. Bowers for his reaction, but the old man handed him back the letter, absorbed in something else.

"Come over here, Willy. There are some new blooms." He was smiling and looking more like his old self. "I'm going to give you some to plant for yourself."

What? Some ole plants? How come?

"I can help you make a window box so you can plant them since you don't have soil in your yard."

"Sure thing, Mr. Bowers," Willy responded, pretending.

Although he'd roamed around Brooklyn during the early part of the summer, he had deliberately avoided a specific street. Not that he'd thought about them much, about the whole business . . . It was just that every once in a while there was a little jab of memory. Now after leaving Mr. Bowers, he headed in the direction of the schoolyard where he'd first seen them.

As he walked, he saw some girls jumping double dutch, and weren't they doing it! Thirty-two, forty-two, fifty-two, not missing a beat. It was fascinating. He stopped to watch. Their feet smashed hard against the pavement. Ninety-two, hundred-two— A miss, he waited for a miss. But the minutes went by. After about ten minutes, one jumper got her feet tangled in the rope. Willy moved on. A man with a shiny-clean head passed, holding up three fingers—the last number for today.

Before he knew it, he was standing directly in front of the gate. Pictures flickered past: the four of them, the ball at his feet—the humiliation, the heat of his shame. He looked through the bars of the gate. There they were inside—the same four? No, too much a co—coincid—how did you say that? A milk crate stood just inside the gate. And Willy decided to go in and sit, to watch.

It had turned out to be a nice day after all. A cool front had moved in to relieve the suffering city people. The hazy sky had burned away into a flawless blue. A gentle breeze kissed his face. Pieces of Sag Harbor drifted back to him. He could almost hear the drone of the crickets. He snapped out of his daydream.

They stood abreast in front of him, frozen as before, the old nightmare repeated. Well, if they tried something, he was going to fight; that's all to it.

A pimpled boy stepped out of the line, closing in. His posture was easy, the ball resting on his left hip. "You one of the Trotters?"

"Me? No—" He was startled. Suddenly it dawned on Willy that they didn't recognize him. They didn't remember him at all!

"I tol' you," the fat boy said, his eyes so swollen they seemed buried in his face. "He's not even wearing their shirt." He went on, "I tol' you we're supposed to meet them in the other yard. We ain't even supposed to be here."

The pimpled boy gestured carelessly. "Okay, okay. Don't scream. I can hear you." But he remained in front of Willy, studying his face.

"Don't I know you from somewhere?"

Willy's forefinger pointed back at himself. He wagged

his head without speaking. The third one drew in from the side. He was shorter than the others. A grin broke across his face, his lips unable to cover his buck teeth. "We know that dude. He's the kid who thought he could play some ball. Couldn't catch, remember?"

The boy directly in front of Willy threw back his head with a burst of laughter. He brought the ball around and faked a throw at Willy. "Ain't learned yet, kid?"

"Shit," uttered Horse Teeth, "you know right well the kid can catch. He's b-a-d, bad as Jabar." Their bodies rocked in ridicule. Nothing had changed. It's the same ole same ole, he told himself, shamed.

"Hey, we ain't got no time to mess with him. We gotta get to the other yard or we'll blow the game. C'mon, let's go!"

Willy sat alone on the crate. The steel grating dug into his behind. He stood up, his energy gone. Why hadn't he jumped stink in their ugly faces, grabbed the ball, and knocked it into their fuckin' guts? Don't matter why. He just didn't.

As he trudged homeward, he kept his eyes on the elongated shadow mocking his body with every step. At the gate, he lifted the latch, noticing how rusted it was before he went inside.

His mother must have just finished on the phone; her hand was still on the receiver. She was so deep in thought that she didn't see Willy come into the room.

Then she noticed him. "Willy. You should have been home sooner. You just missed him."

"Who?" he asked, turning toward her.

"Your father. He wanted to talk to you."

Willy looked at his mother dumbly. Now? He wants to talk to me *now*?

"He left his number," she added. "Maybe you should call right back. He may still be there, wherever that is," she added scornfully.

Willy looked at the piece of paper in his mother's hands. Just a few weeks before, he would've been excited, wide open, ready for Hunt to drop any lie he felt like. He took the paper and began to dial.

"Hello, this is Willy."

"Yeah, say, buddy. I just got off the phone with your mother." Yeah? So what? "I suppose you're kinda pissed, aren't you?"

"No."

"Ah, c'mon, I know you gotta be. But I really got hung up that day. Kept meaning to call you back—just didn't get around to it." Who cares? Who cares?

"Yeah. It's okay."

"No, it *isn't* okay. That's why I called."

Why did he call? To say he's sorry? He sure enough hadn't done that yet. Not that Willy gave a damn. It's too late.

"I know I haven't had the time to be much of a father to you, but you're old enough to understand. The thing is, Willy, I have a whole other kind of life. The hustle, stuff like that there . . . It's just hard to be—" The words were coming fast.

"A father," Willy said with loud sarcasm.

"Now, just hold on—"

117

"No, I don't have to."

His father didn't reply for a long moment. "Maybe you're right. Some of us don't need to be fathers, or husbands either."

"Then don't be none of it!"

He hung up, quite surprised at himself.

## 10

"Okay, Willy, let me see how it looks."

Willy handed Mr. Bowers the wooden box. It sure didn't look too hot—that's for sure. He'd had trouble sawing the wooden planks. The cuts were uneven with little feathery-looking splinters he'd had to file down with sandpaper.

"Now, you're going to paint it. There're some cans of paint in the shed back there. Go on, Willy, choose a color."

Willy gave a silent groan. He sure hated to go into that old shed, climbing over all those boxes, rags, piles of stinking newspapers, and broken lamps. How was he going to find the stupid paint anyway? He let out his breath, making his way across the lawn. Inside, he rummaged around in the dank darkness, stumbling over broken chairs and piles of books.

He found some rusted cans of paint and took one back to Mr. Bowers.

Mr. Bowers read the label, holding the can at arm's length. "Willy, this is white paint. Why would you want to paint your box white?"

Willy scowled. He'd just said to bring some paint. It was enough trouble finding *that*. What difference did it make what color it was? Mr. Bowers was leaning back on his heels, concentrating hard, like he was trying to solve some big ole problem.

"Well, all right. Here's a stick. Stir it up first, and we'll get you some brushes. I think there's coloring in the shed." Oh, no! But Mr. Bowers went off himself to find the colors. Willy picked up a screwdriver and tried to pry open the corroded lid.

His eyes lifted, and he noticed the tree standing tall and straight, its knotted trunk firm and strong. The branches leaned invitingly toward him. While he regarded them idly, he imagined a basketball hoop attached to the trunk. He moved in closer.

Mr. Bowers returned, stopped, and followed Willy's gaze. "What's got your fancy, young fella?"

"The tree . . ."

"The tree? What's wrong with my tree?" He stepped forward, examining the bark.

"No." Willy chuckled. "I was just wondering if I could use it."

"Use it. My tree? For what?" he asked, dumbfounded.

Willy moved closer to the tree. "I like to play basketball, Mr. Bowers," he began, "but I can't play too good. Maybe if I got a basket or something, like, you know, what we use for trash, I could tie it on the tree like a hoop and practice until I can play better."

"Oh, I see." The old man rubbed his gray stubble thoughtfully. "Well, I don't know about that . . . Mrs.

Bowers' room is right here in the back. She's not really well . . ."

"Mr. Bowers . . ." He became more animated. "I won't bother her at all. I'll be real quiet. You remember, right, I don't have a tree in my yard?" But he could tell the old man didn't like the idea. Willy said nothing more and went back to his bucket and began to stir the paint. A fly had dropped into it. He imagined the poor fly trying to escape, frantically struggling for life. He stirred it hard into the thick white river.

"You know, Willy, you would have problems with the ball getting caught up in the tree branches. Let's see . . ." He looked around, his head making small curves in the air. "Tell you what—why don't we put the rim on the side of the shed? It'll be better there, and it's far enough away from the house. And you can't break any of my windows that way," he added mischievously.

"That's a great idea, Mr. Bowers!" Willy exclaimed happily.

"You'll have to find another piece of plywood and some two-by-fours for the backboard." Willy was now glad to go into the old shed.

By afternoon, the box was painted pale lavender, the strongest color the mix offered. It dried on the worktable as they sat talking about how they were going to get a hoop up.

·

As soon as the basket was up, Willy was over in the Bowers' yard all the time, practicing the moves he'd watched on TV. The old man tried to give him some direction, although he knew more about soccer, the kind of football they played on the islands. Things went along pretty well for the next few weeks, and Willy began to feel more confident handling the ball.

Just as he was about to call it quits one afternoon, he looked toward the back of the house. The ball dropped from his hands. Mrs. Bowers was standing in the window, as bald as his basketball! From the open window he could see the wasted body under her loose nightgown.

How long had she been there, her eyes on him like that? Her gaze held him spellbound. Then, suddenly, the lace curtain fell back, and she was gone. For a moment, the empty window made him wonder if he'd imagined the whole thing. Then as he inched a few steps forward, he saw her move back into the darkness. She was a witch! He knew it. He grabbed up the ball and lit out of the yard as fast as his sneakers could carry him.

He could not shake off the sight of Mrs. Bowers and her baldy bean head. Sleep did not come easy that night.

Bertha looked up as Willy grabbed the kitchen chair, scraping it roughly across the tiles before dropping down in it. "What's the matter?"

"Nothing," Willy replied sourly, his eyes lowered.

"It's never nothing, Willy, not when you go around slamming things all over the place."

"Well, it's nothing," he insisted, scowling. Bertha's shoulders lifted in a shrug, and she cracked an egg into the batter.

"And don't make any of that stuff for me," he said, eyeing the Aunt Jemima box.

"What!" she reared back. "I don't believe it. Willy Palmer turning down wheatcakes."

"They make me sleepy."

"Sleepy? I never heard of such a thing."

"Yeah, that's right, especially after you put all that goo on it."

"Oh, the syrup. You forget, you're the one who puts it on there, not me. You put too much. It's the sugar . . ."

She put three cakes on his plate. He looked at them, then away again. "I just blew a job at Shopwell," he said, glowering.

She turned off the jet. "Oh? I didn't know you were looking for a job."

"I wasn't looking for no job," he said, annoyed. "I just saw a sign when I went for the orange juice. I wanted to have some of my own money. I could buy some presents for Kathleen and Jimmy. Send hers by mail . . ."

"Parcel post, I think." Bertha looked at him. "I just wish you'd told me."

"Told you what?"

"That you wanted a job."

"Why?" he asked angrily. He shoved the plate away. "I'm no baby. I know—you figured I wouldn't be able to get a job, right?" he accused her.

"No, I . . ."

"I can't even unload stuff and pile them up in rows, right?"

"Willy . . ." she started, dismayed.

"Oh, I don't want to talk about it!" he shouted. He jumped up, and the chair crashed behind him. Stupid—she still thought he was too stupid for a job!

123

Willy squatted on the stone steps in back of the house, the edge of darkness creeping over the tree, the house opposite, and the shed. At first he ignored Mr. Bowers' call.

"What time are you coming over, Willy? I have to run some errands for my wife later on."

"You go ahead. I'm not coming anyway."

"Why?"

"I just don't feel like it."

He could feel Mr. Bowers was looking at him, but he didn't care. None of his business, anyway. He knew, and probably everybody else knew, he'd never be smart. Why try?

He sat there wondering, thinking things through. Was he really retarded or not? If the word means slow, then he was slow—but only about some things. He'd learned how to swim; he knew all the basketball plays from TV. And if there was something really wrong with him, how could he have known what to do about Jimmy? Retarded people couldn't do things like that. But he still didn't know how to write or read too good. Why? Why couldn't he? He'd seen a story on television about another kid who couldn't read and write—a girl, maybe around Jimmy's age. But she couldn't even talk, or take care of herself. He was nothing like that. Damn near a vegetable, her father had said about his own daughter. A sad story . . . but not him.

Probably been reading good now if Kathleen had stayed. And what about the job? Did he say anything to give himself away? Did he act funny? The man said he needed someone with experience. Just to pile up some boxes? What if he'd said he did have experience, if he'd lied? Then that would be wrong.

Was he a little slow or a lot slow? Would he grow out of it or wouldn't he? Maybe it was just school stuff . . . Everybody don't make it—that's why they're dropouts. But things were getting better—that's for sure. His breath dragged out slowly. Oh, what the hell— Just better get my act together.

## 11

Willy was dismayed by the overcast morning. The clouds were moving quickly together into dark, heavy masses overhead. Another summer storm, and school starting in only a few days. If he didn't go through with this today, it would make the whole summer a shit—and he was going to do it even if it roared thunder and rained down hailstones. He looked back up at the sky, worried. Suppose it did rain? They probably wouldn't show at all. Maybe they weren't even out there today.

Without hurrying, he walked as a light drizzle coated his face. By the time he reached the yard, he was damp and uncomfortable. He inhaled deeply and took four giant steps inside.

"Hi."

They moved toward him slowly, with curiosity. "Well, look what the cat dragged in." Horse Teeth was the first to speak.

"Hey, man, don't you know that them cats ain't got the sense people like to give 'em," Pimpled Boy offered, and everybody cracked up.

He felt his face growing warm, but he was resolved to go to the bitter end, no matter what.

"Throw me the ball," Willy demanded, trying hard to control his cracking voice.

They roared almost in harmony. "Throw what?" "What?" "You kiddin'?"

"Ain't you had enough, kid?" asked Pimpled Boy.

"Can't you see he's whacked?" Fat Boy contributed. "What'cha 'spect?" Willy saw the basketball trapped under Fat Boy's foot. He wanted to turn and bolt, but he held fast. Had to . . .

"You all ain't deaf. I asked you to throw it," Willy said. His voice was strong, but his nerve was sinking fast. Suppose they refused, then what?

"Ay, kid." Fat Boy waved him away and picked up the ball. "Why don't you go back to your mother and have her wipe the snot off your runny nose?"

They giggled like girls, inside their hands. Then they moved into position.

Willy's entire body was aflame. They were not going to throw the ball—they were not going to throw—

"Oh, give him a play. What the hell," Pimpled Boy said all of a sudden.

"What? Fuck that—" Fat Boy was caught by surprise. Quickly he hooked the ball in his arm and backed off a bit. His navel peeped between his T-shirt and the belt of his dungarees.

"What you doing, Wally? Let's have the ball," Pimpled Boy repeated.

"You get nothing!" Fat Boy shot back. "You just better get this kid outta here."

"Oh—so we're going to get into some shit over this, man?"

Fat Boy's face went flabby, his lips loose. Then his face hardened. "I'm down, man." The ball dropped to the pavement as he moved into a defensive stance. "You figure you want to jump in my face over this punk kid, then let's get it on!"

"I wasn't jumping in your face. I just want the ball. I figure maybe the kid's got some guts coming back here. So, give him a chance," Pimpled Boy responded, stepping toward him.

"What the hell for? What do I care about that fuckin' reject!" Fat Boy came in fast, his face pushed up.

Horse Teeth wedged himself between the two. "Nah, y'all crazy? Y'all ain't gonna rumble over some phoney shit like that!"

Fat Boy took advantage, backing off and waving his arms defiantly.

"Don't hold him. Let's get it on!" he yelled.

Horse Teeth pushed them both back. "No, man. Ain't going to be no fighting, and that's all to it."

"This ain't your beef. Be cool." But Willy could see that the fat boy was having second thoughts, wanting to back down.

At that moment, Willy spotted a fourth kid he hadn't noticed before. He was the smallest of the lot, with a round yellow face like a full moon. He wore glasses like Jimmy.

"What's happening?" he asked. "When we going to play some ball?"

"Right now! Let's go." Pimpled Boy called out. Like

the wind, he scooped up the ball, lifted it, and turned toward Willy. Willy readied himself and caught the ball, dribbling to the foul line. He looked steadily at the basket for a long time. Be cool. Be cool. A jump shot, he told himself, try a jump shot. His memory strained back to his nineteen-inch screen. He leaped, let the ball go—and missed.

Maybe he could crawl in a hole and die.

He waited for the jeers. There was only silence. He wiped the water from his face. The drizzle was changing to rain.

"Try it again," someone said. Willy tried again, missing two more times. God—it's bad, real bad. He'd practiced—why?

If he failed this time, it was all over. He positioned himself, looking steadily at the net; then he concentrated with all his might.

He let the ball go. It was through! The empty net fanned the air.

"O-kay!" Willy turned to Horse Teeth, who stood near, arms akimbo. "Dribble to the basket this time and try a lay-up," he told Willy, who followed his directives. Willy retrieved the ball and looked down at it. His hands felt slippery against its pebbled surface. The ball shot up against the backboard and slid off the rim. A stab of disappointment went through him, but there was no stopping now.

He grabbed the ball, dribbled, and it dropped in once again—then twice more. He stared at the swinging net. Then Willy turned triumphantly to face his former tormentors.

He was devastated! Suddenly, as though they had received a secret signal, they'd lost interest. Already turning, they were moving toward the gate.

How— No way! Was that all? But he'd earned a right to their respect, their friendship. He'd worked hard for it. Now, this was all? A choking fury gagged him. He stood alone in the middle of the court. His room—if only he could be in his room right now! The magic carpet, away, away—safe from their put-downs. He knew he was going to cry. No—he couldn't. No crybaby shit, no more—

"Hey! C'mon," said Moon Face over his shoulder. "What'cha waiting for? We gotta go meet the Trotters."

Willy sprang forward to join them. The boy with the moon face and glasses dropped back from the group, waiting for him.

"I'm David," he told Willy as they walked.

"I'm Willy," he responded, pushing his hands in his pockets.

"You looked pretty good out there."

"Nah . . . man, for a minute I thought it was all over."

"You think you got it rough. At least you got the height," David commented, chewing on his bottom lip.

"Which don't mean a thing if you're not used to being out there . . ."

"We just need more practice. You wanna try shooting some together?" he asked casually.

Willy darted a look at him, realizing how much the kid reminded him of Jimmy. "That'll be great!" Then he noticed how far ahead the group was getting. "We'll rap on it later; we'd better catch up." Not until that moment did he realize the rain had stopped.

A cool wind nipped at Willy's nose as he stepped out on the sidewalk, heading home. Yep, the summer was just about gone—'cept for Indian summer, which would happen sometime, but you never knew when it would show up. And in a couple more weeks the leaves would lose their green, and each tree would choose its own color.

The night before, his mother had told him she'd found a vocational school for him. He didn't know . . . you still had to know how to read instructions and stuff. Well, no use worrying about that now. Actually, what he really wished he could do was go to the islands and work with the men who picked bananas. Sweating in the sun. Good ole sweat, and don't nobody have to have any brains for that.

Bet there would be tests in this school, too. There would probably be tests all of his life. Failing tests. Maybe sometimes he'd pass, like he did this summer. You can't help what you don't have anyway—that's for sure. Just gotta make the best of it.

He looked up at the window where he'd seen the bald-headed Mrs. Bowers and saw the shades drawn. He had a feeling the house was empty. They're probably at the clinic. He wondered how Aunt Bessie was doing. He'd have to make a trip back before school started. Jimmy's parents had invited him and his mother out for the weekend. It would be good to see Jimmy again, catch the last of the sun and water.

He saw his ball sitting in front of the screen door and

strolled over to pick it up. He flung it hard against the side of the house and it came back, a flying disk as it returned, gold in the sunlight. And Willy wondered, just for a moment, if a girl in a sheer print dress, her feet bare, was gazing into the same sun from that place that never had winter.